Story of the year

the ten winning stories

THE INDEPENDENT

Story of the year

the ten winning stories

*Rosamund Annetts, Simon Cheshire,
Fiona Gibson, Geoffrey Henderson,
Sara Mason, Nicola Muntzer,
John Nevinson, Janet Frances Smith,
Jenny Swanson, B.J. Weir.*

The Federation of Children's Book Groups

SCHOLASTIC

Scholastic Children's Books,
Commonwealth House, 1–19 New Oxford Street,
London WC1A 1NU, UK
a division of Scholastic Ltd
London ~ New York ~ Toronto ~ Sydney ~ Auckland

Published in the UK by Scholastic Ltd, 1998

ISBN: 0 590 11328 3

Typeset by DP Photosetting, Aylesbury, Bucks.
Printed by Cox & Wyman Ltd., Reading, Berks

2 4 6 8 10 9 7 5 3

Contents

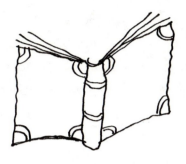

Introduction

It's that time of year again! For the sixth year running, Scholastic Children's Books and the *Independent* have combined forces to bring you 1998's top ten stories for six- to nine-year-olds.

- The winners this year were gleaned from over one thousand entries and the quality was just as high as in previous years. There was much fun to be had choosing them and several arguments as well! It's never an easy job, but in the end the stories were whittled down to twenty-two, from which the magic ten were chosen. The lucky people with that rewarding task were a panel of six judges: Tony Jordan, script-writer for *East-Enders* and *City Central*; Anne Finnis, freelance editor; David Fickling, Publishing Director of

Scholastic Children's Books; Suzanne Moore, columnist for the *Independent*; Trish Botten, Librarian; and Jo Williams of the Federation of Children's Book Groups – an organization which promotes children's books and reading. She represented children from seven schools who read the shortlist, and their votes counted towards the final decision.

And what a lightning-quick decision it was! There was no beating about the bush as *Toebiter* literally grabbed the judges to become this year's outright winner. A chucklesome, stinky tale of everyday under-the-bed scariness, it's sure to have *you* checking for any bedtime critters. The two runners up are also real smashers. The naughty, thought-provoking *Little King Who Broke Things* and the very real birthday let-downs of *Uncle George's Magic Painting Set* will ring true for both children and adults alike. All the stories included in this book are unique little gems in their own right and reflect storytelling at its most original and exciting. Accompanied, as ever, by beautiful pictures from top-of-the-crop illustrators, this is a collection to revisit again and again.

INTRODUCTION

There's nothing like the thrill of publishing fresh, new talent and this is what *Story of the Year* is dedicated to. So, with every one a winner, please dive in and find *your* favourite story of the year.

Scholastic Children's Books

Winner

Toebiter

Nicola Muntzer

Illustrated by
Valeria Petrone

"*Toebiter, toebiter, under my bed,*
    If you bite me tonight, I'll kick off your
    head.
You may try and hide, but I know you are there,
So I'll pull off your ears and I'll tear out your hair.

Toebiter, toebiter, don't you dare
Show your teeth and give me a scare..."

"Katie Maclaren, stop talking to yourself and get into bed."

But Katie Maclaren wasn't talking to herself. She was talking to *it* – the unseen thing that lurked beneath her bed, the thing that had come to live in that dark, scary gap where the mattress ended and the floor began. Nor could she suddenly break off halfway through this special

13

warning curse or the toebiter would know she was scared of it. And the one thing you must never do is let a toebiter know you are scared. They feed on fear, along with tiny drops of blood from soft young human toes.

Katie shut her eyes tight, screwed her hands up into two hard fists and gabbled the rest of the curse under her breath.

"... *If I feel your teeth sinking into my toes, I'll punch you hard on your very long nose. So there!*"

"Katie – bed – NOW!"

There was a rush of air as Katie leapt, a twang of protesting bed springs as she landed on the mattress, followed by a sob of relief. She had escaped. Beneath the bed she thought she heard the toebiter grinding his teeth in frustrated fury. It was a small unpleasant sound, rather like the rasping of two pennies rubbing together. Suddenly it was replaced by a short devilish chuckle. Katie's heart sank. She knew the toebiter might have missed her tonight but it would get her tomorrow.

Most people can find something unexpected under their bed, even if it's only a wisp of fluff, a forgotten paper hanky or a stray marble, but no one that Katie knew of had anything even half as terrifying as a toebiter. The worst that any of her friends had found was a spider, and you can get rid of spiders. Toebiters are not so easy. They cling invisibly to the springs or the underside of the mattress like a headlouse clings to a shaft of hair. When threatened, they ooze silently between the cracks in the floorboards or they creep craftily into the doll's house and watch through the miniature windows until it is safe to come out. So, naturally, when Katie told her parents about the toebiter and they moved her bed to hoover underneath, there was no sign of anything nasty.

"There!" they said triumphantly, switching the hoover off. "That's got rid of the nasty gnome for you."

"It's not a gnome."

"Goblin then."

"It's not a goblin either."

"What is it then?" Katie's father was getting restless. There was a big match on in five minutes and he wanted to be there, in front of the TV before it started.

"It's a toebiter," Katie explained. "A brown one."

"Whatever it is," he said, pointing to the freshly cleaned carpet, "it's gone now. See..."

Katie did see. It was obvious that grown-ups were pretty thick when it came to toebiters. They did not realize that toebiters are clever creatures and don't just lounge around waiting to be hoovered up. The toebiter was so crafty that even Katie herself had never seen it. But she did not need to actually clap eyes on it to know what it looked like and the toebiter looked like nothing she had ever seen before. Its body was small and hairy, but its head, mushrooming from a squat, wrinkled neck, was large, lumpy and hairless. It had no need of eyes, living as it did in dark, secret places so, where its eyes should have been, there were only two horrible sightless mounds. Its nose, on the other hand, was highly developed. Sensitive and boneless, it probed and wiggled, homing in on human flesh as an earthworm pushes blindly through soil towards the light. And when human flesh was sniffed out, the toebiter would pounce, using long rubbery arms to seize its prey and a mouth full of razor-sharp yellow teeth to draw blood. But the worst thing about the toebiter, worse even than its worm-like nose or its tiny grasping claws or its brown wizened body, was its smell.

Sometimes the smell wafting out from under Katie's bed was overpowering. It was a combination of all the most disgusting pongs imaginable – a freshly opened packet of peanuts, burnt toast, blue cheese, cat poo, steaming nappies, Brussels sprouts on the boil, kippers, week-old football socks and breath of dog. But the annoying thing was, only Katie seemed able to smell it. There had been a ray of hope one morning when her mother had paused while tucking Katie's sheets in and sniffed suspiciously.

"Phew, what's that stink?" she had demanded, rummaging under Katie's bed.

"Toebiter," said Katie.

"Toebiter, my foot." And Mrs Maclaren had smiled, seized something lying under the bed and tossed it straight into the waste-paper bin. "If you must eat bananas in your room," she had continued, "at least throw the skin away afterwards."

Katie had stared at her mother incredulously.

Couldn't she smell it? Couldn't she smell toe-biter? Would no one ever believe her?

Then, one day at school, they had to write about the most frightening thing in the world. Katie, naturally, described the toebiter and the teacher was so impressed with her story that he read it aloud to the class. And at playtime, a boy called Nathan Spong came up to Katie.

"This toebiter thing. . ." he said, "I can get rid of it for you."

Now, Nathan Spong was not known for his clever ideas. In fact, people made fun of him because his hair grew straight up from his scalp in a rather surprised way and because of his name. (There are several words that rhyme with Spong and none of them are nice, but Katie was desperate.)

"Can you really get rid of it?" she asked.

"I think so." He paused. "Do you want it captured alive?"

"No!"

"Dead then," Nathan nodded. "In that case, we need to work out what likes to eat toebiters. Everything in the world has a predator, something or somebody that likes to hunt it and eat it.

I can't see a toebiter being any different. Unless ... you don't think it comes from another planet or something?"

"No-o. I think it crawled up from the compost heap," Katie said.

"That's good. I'm not sure I can do aliens. Now, we need to know what a toebiter tastes like in order to work out what would want to eat it." Nathan took out a jotter and a pencil stub and looked expectantly at Katie.

"I'm not sure how it tastes," she said thoughtfully, "but it smells revolting – not like anything we'd want to eat anyway."

Nathan made a note of this, then asked a few more questions: was it tame? Would it fit into a matchbox? Was it vicious? Katie answered as best she could until finally, he put his pencil and jotter away.

"Leave it with me," he said mysteriously. "You ask me to tea on Wednesday and I'll see what I can do... I like sausage and chips by the way."

And on Wednesday after school, as promised, Nathan Spong turned up on Katie's doorstep clutching a shoebox under one arm and a small, dirty white dog under the other. "Grubber can wait in the garden," Nathan said, "while we're busy."

But Grubber did not like being shut out in the garden and Katie heard him whining and scrabbling at the back door while she and Nathan climbed the stairs with the shoebox. She was not allowed to look inside this box. "I do experiments," he told her darkly. "Top secret ones. This –" he patted the box – "is highly confidential."

From her bed, Katie watched as, very slowly and carefully, Nathan loosened the lid of the shoebox. He pushed the box slowly towards the gap under the bed, turned it gingerly on to its side, gave it a tap, then leapt up on to the bed next to Katie.

"What happens now?" she whispered.

"We give it three and a half minutes exactly," Nathan whispered back. "Then we see if it's worked."

Three and a half minutes seems an eternity when you are waiting for something out of the ordinary to happen. Katie watched the second hand crawl around the face of her alarm clock –

twenty seconds ... thirty seconds ... thirty-five seconds ... forty ... one minute... She peered over the edge of the bed at the upturned shoe-box, watching and waiting with bated breath. She could hear her heart thumping loudly and Nathan breathing heavily with concentration beside her... One minute passed ... one minute and thirty seconds ... thirty-five ... forty... From the kitchen downstairs came the muffled clatter of pots and pans as Mr Maclaren began preparing tea... Two minutes... In the garden, Grubber had stopped whining and scrabbling and was whimpering quietly. There was no sound from either the box or the toebiter... Two minutes and twenty seconds ... thirty ... forty...

"Time's up." Nathan's voice made Katie jump. "Ready?"

She nodded. Together they took off their shoes and socks and lowered their bare feet over the edge of the bed until their toes were dangling temptingly in the gap where the toebiter lurked.

"I can smell it," Katie said fearfully. A reek of rotten fish and cheesy socks seeped into the room. The gap beneath the bed remained omi-nously silent. A small breath of air tickled the soles of Katie's feet. She snatched them back up quickly to safety but Nathan was more confident.

"Seems to have worked." He wriggled his toes recklessly. "I think my experiment was successful – yeowch!" As he spoke, his whole body shot up into the air and landed back on the bed in a huddle. He turned white, then pink, then white again and there, on the second toe of his left foot was the distinct impression of two sharp little teeth. He rubbed at the tiny marks with shock and disbelief.

"It bit me," he said in surprise. "It actually bit me."

Katie was about to reply that biting toes was what toebiters actually did, when she heard a commotion downstairs. The kitchen door burst open and, over a background noise of sizzling sausages, came a yell, "Come back here you little—" from Katie's dad. This was followed directly by a sound like a herd of stampeding antelope galloping up the stairs and a very unantelope-like panting.

"Grubber," Nathan groaned, "you were supposed to stay outside."

But Grubber the dog had other ideas. Yelping with excitement, he charged towards the gap under Katie's bed. Flat on his belly, he squirmed and wriggled until almost all of his body had disappeared underneath the bed and only his tail, wagging furiously, remained visible. Snap! Snap! His jaws met, missing their target, but on the third snap came a sickening crunching, slurping noise and a single thin, high-pitched screech. Then nothing.

Katie looked at Nathan. Nathan looked at Katie. And Grubber, backing out from under the bed, glanced from one to the other, licking his lips and looking very pleased with himself.

The dog sat for a moment, quite still on the rug in front of them, and as he sat, a low rumble began deep in his belly. At first the rumble was no more than a distant growl, but as it started to move, creeping upwards, it grew louder and louder until, by the time it was vibrating in Grubber's throat, it had become thunderous. Katie and Nathan stared at him, transfixed. Grubber closed his eyes, opened his mouth and let out an enormous ... BELCH. The smell that escaped with the enormous belch was absolutely atrocious – a combination of freshly opened packets of peanuts, burnt toast, blue cheese, cat poo, steaming nappies, Brussels sprouts on the boil, kippers, week-old football socks and breath of dog – atrocious but instantly recognizable.

Toebiter.

A species now – thanks to a small dirty white dog named Grubber – extinct.

NICOLA MUNTZER

Nicola Muntzer was born in Epsom, Surrey, but now lives in Selsey, West Sussex. With her job as a domestic and care assistant in an old people's home, and two daughters aged six and eight, she is kept very busy indeed. But Nicola still manages to find time to write, which is her favourite pastime. Toe-biter is one of the first stories she has written for children.

She says: "I read to my own two children every night, so I have a good idea of what appeals to them. They love to be frightened, so long as good conquers bad in the end. Both the title and the list of smells associated with the toebiter were suggested to me by my eldest daughter. I have found also that there is a wide range of reading abilities in this age group and with adults often having to read aloud to children, I felt the story had to appeal to them as well."

Runner-up

The Little King
Who Broke Things

GEOFFREY HENDERSON

Illustrated by
NICK SHARRATT

Once, long ago, there was a king and his name was Simon. He was a good king. He ruled a little kingdom of high mountains and grassy fields and just one town.

Every Christmas, King Simon invited all the children to his castle for a party and he gave presents to everyone. The king had a son whose name was Hubert. Hubert broke things.

Anyone might break something accidentally and usually they are sorry about it afterwards, but Hubert broke things for the fun of it, and to attract attention to himself. He broke all his toys as soon as he got them. He twisted and he tore, he bent and he dented, he pulled and he pushed, he prized and he parted, he unwound, unhooked, unscrewed, and undid, he bashed, walloped, and biffed. The way he managed to break things was really amazing.

When he had finished breaking all his toys, his mother, the queen, sent for more.

"I wouldn't give him anything," said King Simon. "He's a naughty boy."

"He'll grow out of it," replied the queen, and she went away for a while because Hubert was crying and she didn't like the sound of crying very much.

One day he threw the royal mace – which was made of gold and studded with diamonds – out of a window into the moat.

King Simon was terribly angry. "Send him to bed without his supper," he said.

But his mother, the queen, said, "He'll grow out of it."

When Christmas arrived and it was time for King Simon's party, all the children came to the castle to eat cakes and jellies and to get their presents. King Simon was never more happy than when he was giving presents to children and watching them laugh and play. But Hubert spoiled everything.

He was rude to the little girls and made them

cry so that their mothers had to take them home because they knew that the queen didn't like the sound of crying. He started fights with the other boys and then ran and told the queen that it was their fault and not his.

It wasn't worth going to the king's party while Hubert was there, and of course he was always there, so nobody came at all!

King Simon was very upset. He took off his crown and put on his long woollen night cap; he lit a little candle and he went to bed.

"He has made me very unhappy," said the king as he wound his way slowly up the stone staircase to his bedroom. "He's a naughty little boy."

"He'll grow out of it," said the queen, and she patted Hubert on the head. Hubert put his arms around his mother's skirts and sucked his thumb – thoughtfully.

But Hubert did not grow out of it, and when good King Simon died, little Hubert became king.

"What can you do about a bad king?" sighed the Lord High Chamberlain, and all the ministers looked at the Minister of Ideas because he was supposed to have the best ideas.

The Minister of Ideas leant back in his chair and scratched the top of his head. Then he leant forward and buried his face in his hands. He stood up and looked down at the floor. Then he sat down again and looked up at the ceiling. He put out the tip of his tongue and then put it back in again. Then, when it seemed that he was going to have an idea, he took a deep breath and said, "I don't know."

"Stop his Saturday sweets," said the Minister of Pocket Money.

"Give him dry bread for his supper," said the Secretary of State for Cakes and Jellies.

"Multiply his division and add his subtraction," suggested the Minister of Arithmetic who was very old and wore a long beard.

"It means making a law," said the Lord High Chamberlain. "And he'll break that just as does with everything else."

The Minister of Swings and Roundabouts brought his fist down on the great council table so violently that everyone stopped talking instantly. "Lock him up in the castle and don't let him out," he said in a deep dark voice.

They all agreed that while it was a harsh thing to do, it was necessary for the sake of the kingdom. Right away, the Lord High Chamberlain wrote out a proclamation in his best handwriting which said:

Hear ye! Hear ye!
King Hubert is to be locked
in the castle
and not to be let out.
By order of the Lord High Chamberlain.

Then they took the proclamation up to the castle and nailed it to the big front door.

The bootboy saw the notice and he told the scullery maid, who told the footmen, who went to tell the butler. The butler told the cook and she was in such a hurry to tell the ladies-in-waiting that she let the milk boil over. The ladies-in-waiting told the queen. When the queen heard about the proclamation she said, "It will only upset him and make him cry. I have a dreadful headache," and she went to bed. "Go and tell

King Hubert about it," she said, and she put her hand over her eyes and sighed deeply.

The ladies-in-waiting told the cook to tell the king but the cook said that the butler should tell him. The butler told the footmen to tell the king and the footmen sent the scullery maid to do it. The scullery maid told the bootboy that the queen said he must tell King Hubert that he was to be kept in and not allowed out of the castle. Although the bootboy's work was to clean all the boots and shoes, he nearly always had to do the things nobody else felt like doing, so he went to tell the king.

Hubert was in his playroom and was about to break a beautiful wooden railway engine that he had found in a corner of a cupboard.

"They're going to lock you up for ever," said the bootboy. "There's a notice about it on the front door."

Hubert tugged a wheel off the engine. "They can't lock me up because I'm the king," he said, and he pulled another wheel off.

The bootboy had never seen such a fine toy. It was red and green and it had a tall black chimney. There was a whistle and a big light and a thing on the front for pushing cows off the line. The wheels were black with gold scrolls. The bootboy had watched his father carving wooden things to be used on the farm and he knew how difficult it was to make such a beautiful toy.

"Watch me pull this to pieces," said Hubert, and his eyes sparkled with joy as he pulled and twisted until it was all broken into bits which he promptly threw out of the window.

When King Hubert went to leave the castle to get more toys, he knew that what the bootboy had told him was true and he was locked in. He cried all day and screamed so loudly that the white doves in the courtyard were so startled they flew up into the air and never came back. He jumped up and down, he kicked and he stamped, he shrieked and he shouted: "How dare they lock up the king!"

The queen put her hands to her ears and hurried away to see another queen on the other side of the mountains. The ladies-in-waiting went with the queen. Cook said that she had to visit a sick aunt in the country, and all the footmen went with her to carry her bags. The butler suddenly remembered that he had

forgotten to ask Cook about Sunday lunch, and he scurried after her as fast as he could.

Then the big castle became very, very quiet...

When Hubert saw the empty chairs left about with nobody sitting in them and things left undone where they were because everyone had gone in such a hurry, he began to feel afraid and alone.

But Hubert was not alone; the bootboy had not gone. He had wrapped up his few possessions in a big blue handkerchief and he was about to follow the butler when he had a thought ... and he stayed behind.

"Never mind," said the bootboy. "We can light the fire in the great hall and sit around and tell stories."

"Don't want to tell stories," replied Hubert moodily, and he went out into the courtyard. Autumn had just laid all the golden-brown leaves on the ground and Hubert kicked sulkily through them. Then he sat down in a big pile of leaves and looked sad and small.

"I never felt more like breaking something and I haven't got anything to break," he said to the bootboy.

As they both walked back into the castle, Hubert kicked the leaves because he was cross. Suddenly the bootboy saw something almost hidden; it was one of the wheels of the wooden engine that Hubert had just broken. He picked it up and said, "I've an idea." And he began searching amongst the leaves. "We've got to find all the pieces of the engine," said the bootboy.

"Why?" asked Hubert.

"I'll tell you why when we've found every piece," replied the bootboy.

The bootboy was so enthusiastic that Hubert couldn't help joining in the search. Together they ran against the wind and the leaves scattered into the air and, when they had found the last piece – the tall black chimney – the sun came out for a moment and sent rays of golden light through the clouds into the courtyard.

"Come with me," said the bootboy, and he went to the back of the castle where there was a room used by the men who had to look after the building. Inside, there were all kinds of tools for carpentry neatly racked along the walls.

The bootboy put all the parts of the toy engine on the bench and said, "I shall put it back together again and then you will have something to break. And every time you break it, I will mend it. And then you will be happy."

"Oh, what a wonderful idea!" exclaimed Hubert. "Mend it right away."

The bootboy carefully hammered back the wheels and the cabin for the driver, and the thing for pushing cows off the rails, and the big light. Finally, the only part left was the tall black chimney.

"I want to do the chimney part," said Hubert. The bootboy showed the king how to use the hammer and, though he was afraid that Hubert would hit his fingers, in the end the chimney was replaced – though it was just a little wobbly.

"There you are," said the bootboy, holding the engine proudly. "Now you can break it up again."

"Well … you see…" mumbled King Hubert. "It *is* very beautiful, and I do like breaking things … but … could we leave it until tomorrow?"

When tomorrow came, it began to snow. It was just the sort of day when Hubert would have done nothing but break things. He and the bootboy went to the carpentry room and stayed quiet for a while, looking at the engine.

"Now you can break it to pieces," said the bootboy.

King Hubert shuffled his feet and scratched the back of his neck. Then he shrugged his shoulders and said, "Humm". Then he gave the engine a little push and the big wheels turned, and the chimney wobbled a little, and you could easily imagine the whistle blowing and the steam puffing out in a white cloud as it all went clickety clack on its way. King Hubert said, "Humm" again and then suddenly, "Let's see if there are any other toys we can put back together."

And that is how this part of the story began.

It was five days before Christmas, and the Lord High Chamberlain had planned *his* grand party. But the people remembered good King Simon's parties and they knew that the Lord High Chamberlain's party wouldn't really be much fun. They said to themselves sadly, "If only Hubert hadn't spoiled it all."

Meanwhile extraordinary things had been happening in the castle. Where there had been piles of broken toys, there were now wonderful things to be seen.

"Whatever are we going to do with them?" said King Hubert.

"Let's have a party and give everyone a toy," said the bootboy.

"They won't come because they know how horrid I was. Who would believe that I don't break things any more?"

"We'll show them!" said the bootboy firmly. "We'll show them in the big castle window."

So the bootboy and King Hubert arranged all the toys in the castle window and Hubert wrote out a notice which said:

ROYAL CHRISTMAS PARTY
Everyone will get a toy.
I DON'T BREAK THINGS ANY MORE
AND I PROMISE TO BE GOOD.
signed, Hubert, king

When the people saw the notice, a wave of mutterings went round the town. There were whisperings in the doorways and there were head-shakings and head-noddings, and there were yes's and no's and maybe's everywhere.

On Christmas Day the Lord High Chamberlain stood at the door of his house waiting for everyone to come to his party. But the people had decided that it was only fair to give King Hubert a chance and they all went up to the castle. The Minister of Arithmetic was the only one who arrived at the Lord High Chamberlain's party.

The Lord High Chamberlain put on his big overcoat which he buttoned up the wrong way, and put his squirrel hat on with the tail the wrong way round so it tickled his nose, and he wore his overshoes on the wrong feet and hobbled up to the castle.

It was a wonderful party. Everyone got a present and King Hubert was so good that all the mothers said in little whispers, "What a good king he is going to be."

And they were right; King Hubert became as good a king as his father, King Simon, had been. When Hubert's mother, the queen, heard that Hubert didn't cry so much, she came back to live in the castle and King Hubert was always kind to her. The bootboy became Lord High Chamberlain. Best of all, King Hubert's kingdom became famous everywhere for making beautiful toys. And on the State Coat of Arms there is a toy train with a big black chimney and wheels with gold scrolls.

The old Lord High Chamberlain was given a holiday for as long as he lived and a pension of one hundred chocolates a week. For something to do, he began to write the history of the Kingdom. He wrote this story.

GEOFFREY HENDERSON

Geoffrey Henderson has lived all over the world and has had an even more colourful career. He has been an RAF pilot, an assistant stage manager, a police Lieutenant in the Malay Police and in 1976 was called to the Bar to practise employment law. He has also invented a device to deal with jet lag, but now concentrates on writing full time! He's had a short story published in the London Magazine *in 1997 and has won two awards for his writing. One was first prize in the Kent Literary Festival for short stories and the other was first prize for the Robert Morley Competition for television scripts. He also writes poetry and is in the middle of writing a novel. He has two grown up children and lives in Kent. He believes that the older he gets, the better he understands how young children think.*

Runner-up

Uncle George's Magic Painting Set

FIONA GIBSON

Illustrated by
AILIE BUSBY

Allie and Eddie were waiting for their baby to come. Every week, as Allie's tummy grew bigger, Eddie opened a book about babies and told Allie what it said. "This week," read Eddie, "the baby is as big as an olive."

An olive? That didn't sound very big. From the way she couldn't stop eating, Allie had imagined a huge, greedy pumpkin in there.

Allie's was no ordinary hunger. She wanted weird, mismatched things – things that didn't usually go together. For breakfast, for instance, Allie would have something sweet like strawberries (with pickled onions). For lunch, she'd have something savoury like spaghetti (with rice pudding). For dinner, she'd really go bananas and ask Eddie for a bowl of marshmallows (with mustard).

"I'm worried about you," said Eddie, when Allie demanded tuna (with toffee) before she went to bed.

"I can't help it," said Allie, and she couldn't. All she could think about was food, food, food, in peculiar combinations. "Perhaps it's the little fella," she said, giving her tummy a tap.

The following week, Eddie consulted the book about babies. "This week," he told Allie, "the baby is the size of a plum."

A plum? That didn't sound very big. By now, Allie was squeezing in extra meals between ordinary meals: chocolate (with gherkins) mid-morning, and crackers (with custard) in the early afternoon. Sometimes she woke in the night and sneaked downstairs to the freezer. She'd take a tub of vanilla ice-cream, dip in a spoon and whisper, "Mmm. I fancy a fried egg with that."

The following week, Eddie opened the book about babies to see if it said anything about eating funny things together. "The baby is now the size of a large lime," he read. A large lime? That didn't sound very big. Allie's tummy now filled her biggest red sweater and stuck out so far that she couldn't see her feet. She looked like a giant tomato. That day, Eddie took his giant tomato by the hand and led her to the hospital. They had an appointment with Dr Chang to check that the baby was growing well.

"Blimey," said Dr Chang, staring at Allie's sticky-out belly. "Let's see what's going on in there."

Dr Chang showed Allie and Eddie into a small, darkened room full of bleeping equipment. The only lights came from flickering machines. Eddie perched on a plastic chair and Allie lay on a little bed. "Well," said Dr Chang. "Are you ready to see your baby?"

He turned on a screen that looked just like a telly. Eddie stared at it, wondering what their baby would look like. Allie lay very quiet and still. She was hungry. Did she fancy something sweet or savoury? She couldn't decide. Suddenly, the TV screen sprang to life. At first they couldn't see a baby – just swirling specks like hailstones. Allie and Eddie waited. Allie's tummy growled so loudly it sounded like a train rumbling under the hospital.

"There it is!" said Dr Chang. He pointed at a tiny blob on the screen. It was curled up like a frightened caterpillar. "And there," said Dr Chang, "is the other one."

The other one? Allie and Eddie stared. Two curled-up caterpillars. Twins!

"So," laughed Eddie, "that's why you've been eating so much!"

As the months went by, Allie's belly swelled so big that Eddie had to squeeze her into the car. She had in-between meals between in-between meals, and in-between snacks between those. When the babies were ready to be born, Eddie helped Allie waddle into hospital.

The babies were born in the middle of the night, and Allie and Eddie held one each. "Look," said Allie. "Two boys. Aren't we lucky?" They decided to call them Dexter and Sam, and wondered how on earth they'd tell them apart.

Dexter had long, kicky legs and serious brown eyes. Sam had long, kicky legs and serious brown eyes. Allie and Eddie's friends and family clustered round the hospital bed to look. "Incredible," they marvelled, examining each baby in turn. "They're absolutely identical."

Each visitor brought presents. Allie unwrapped two blue sweaters, two red jackets and two yellow hats with pompons on top. An elderly auntie had even knitted two green rompers with zips up the front. "They look like pea pods," laughed Eddie.

"Peas in a pod," said the auntie. "They're twins, after all."

Dexter and Sam stared at the presents with serious brown eyes. If everyone had stopped yacking for a moment, they might have noticed Dexter heave a sigh and Sam drum impatient fingers on the side of his cot. But they didn't, because everyone was blethering so much.

It was almost the end of visiting time when Uncle George arrived. He was quieter than the rest of the mob, and handed Allie two tiny parcels. Inside each was a vest: one with a fish on the front, for Sam, and one with a tiger on the front, for Dexter.

"Different presents for twins?" laughed Eddie. "You are funny, Uncle George."

Allie and Eddie took their brand new boys

home from hospital. As the months went by, Sam and Dexter guzzled so much milk and slurped so much squidgy baby food that they grew plumper and taller until they weren't babies any more.

"They're doing well, aren't they?" Allie asked Eddie one evening. Only one thing worried her. Everyone agreed that the boys were identical, yet they didn't behave identically at all. If Allie dressed Dexter in his blue sweater, Sam would thrash his long, kicky legs and refuse to put his blue sweater on. If Sam was wearing his red jacket, Dexter would throw himself on to the floor, roaring and bellowing until his red jacket was taken away and hidden in a cupboard.

Mealtimes were difficult too. Sam liked sweet, sloppy things like custard, porridge and banana. Dexter liked munchy, crunchy things like green beans, broccoli and biscuits. Whatever Sam liked, Dexter didn't. And whatever Dexter liked, Sam didn't. If Allie or Eddie gave either boy the wrong thing to eat, they would hammer on their high chairs and fling down their spoons.

"They're serious boys, aren't they?" said friends and family, politely. "Don't they like our presents?"

Dexter and Sam didn't say anything. They just stared at their presents with serious brown eyes.

On their first birthday they got:
identical pairs of tartan dungarees
identical cuddly koalas
identical sets of wooden building blocks
identical velvet penguins that peeped when you
    pressed them.

On their second birthday they got:
identical red tricycles (with trailers)
identical pairs of yellow wellies
identical cream-coloured sweaters
identical farm sets with pigs, cows and
    sheep dogs.

On their third birthday they got:
identical bikes with stabilizers
identical garages with ramps for cars to go up
    and down

identical cassette players with songs to sing
  along to
identical books with hard, shiny covers.

"What's your book about, Sam?" asked Dexter.

"Goblins and monsters," said Sam. "What's yours about?"

"Goblins and monsters," said Dexter. They stared at each other with serious brown eyes. They hardly played with their toys that day.

And so the years went on. Twins share a birthday and double birthdays mean double presents. One year, Sam would open his presents first, and Dexter would go second. The next year Dexter would go first, and Sam would go second. But they weren't excited. They were never excited. Because they knew that whatever Sam had, Dexter would have too. And whatever Dexter had, Sam would have too.

It was on their seventh birthday that Uncle George popped by with two large gifts. Sam's was a painting set. Dexter's was a painting set. "Identical painting sets for identical boys," said Allie, smiling. "Won't you say thanks to Uncle George?"

"Thanks, Uncle George," said Dexter, quietly.

"Thanks, Uncle George," said Sam, glumly.

Uncle George put his coat on. "Enjoy them," he said, raising one of his old, grey eyebrows. "They're not ordinary painting sets."

For the rest of the day, Sam and Dexter played with their presents. "What kind of cars did you get?" asked Sam.

"A tractor, a sports car and a milk float," said Dexter.

"Whoop-di-doop," said Sam. "Me too."

Secretly, though, Sam felt guilty. There was nothing wrong with their presents. The milk float even had churns that fitted on top. Maybe they should be grateful that people had even remembered their birthday.

Dexter felt bad too. After all, Uncle George's painting sets were pretty impressive, with easels, brushes and twenty-five different colours of paint. Sam and Dexter each pinned paper on to their easels and, in perfect silence, began to paint. Allie watched through a crack in the kitchen door, glad to see her boys enjoying a birthday at last. For two and a half hours, Sam and Dexter painted, stopping only to grab a quick snack of chicken drumsticks (Dexter) and banana milk-shake (Sam).

By the time Eddie came home from work, the boys had just finished. Eddie stopped and looked around the room. Dribbles of orange trickled from the easels on to the carpet. A splatter of yellow daubed the lamp shade. Dexter had smears of purple on his forehead; Sam had green on one eyebrow. Eddie put down his briefcase. He opened his mouth to shout like mad dads did, but only air came out. What were they thinking, wrecking the house? What was Allie thinking, letting them run riot?

"Allie—" he began.

"Shhh," whispered Allie. "They've been painting all afternoon. It's the first time they've enjoyed a birthday, so don't spoil it."

Eddie shrugged. So what had the artists been up to? First, Eddie looked at Sam's easel. He expected something simple like a tree or a dog or a flower. But what he saw was this: a vivid ocean scene with waves of blue and green. Tiny gold flecks lit the waves like sunlight. Brilliant orange fish dipped and dived between the currents.

From the bottom of the ocean, tangled plants grew, and crabs lurked between pebbles. "Wow," said Eddie. "That's some painting, my boy."

He turned to Dexter's painting. It would be an ocean scene too, of course, perhaps with different fish; after all, Sam and Dexter were twins, and twins would paint similar pictures. Eddie looked at Dexter's easel. There, to his amazement, was an incredible jungle scene. Tall, strong grasses sprang from the earth, reaching to a piercing blue sky. And, between the undergrowth, tigers lurked, searching out prey with their glinting yellow eyes. "Wow," said Eddie. "I never knew you two could be so different."

Eddie was so pleased with the paintings that he framed them and hung them on the living-room wall. Whenever friends and family came to visit, they would ask the usual questions:

"Are Dexter and Sam alike?"

"Do they do the same things?"

"How on earth can you tell them apart?"

Eddie and Allie would point at the paintings of the ocean and the jungle and say, "Make up your own minds about that."

People stopped asking dumb questions. And on Sam and Dexter's eighth birthday they got:

(Dexter)
a kit to make a helicopter
a T-shirt with planets on the front
a robot whose tummy opened to show the
    machinery
a kite shaped like a tiger
a book about dinosaurs;
(Sam)
a kit to make a Spitfire plane
six colours of modelling clay
a kite shaped like a fish
a rucksack with secret zip-up compartments
a book about spiders and insects.

Sam and Dexter no longer gave people long, serious stares. They played with their presents, and played with each other's, and swapped and compared until Allie said it was really, truly, honestly time for bed.

Late that night, they lay in bed, waiting for sleep to creep over them. Dexter munched a biscuit he'd hidden under the covers. Sam

nibbled a banana he'd stashed beneath his pillow.

"What a birthday," whispered Dexter from
his bed.

"The best ever," whispered Sam. "And you
know who we should really thank?"

"Uncle George," whispered Dexter.

"Thanks, Uncle George," whispered Sam.

FIONA GIBSON

Fiona Gibson grew up in a small Yorkshire village called Goose Eye. She now lives in London with her husband Jimmy and twin boys Sam and Dexter. Her first job was writing horoscopes for Jackie *magazine and from then she went on to bigger and better things. These included Beauty Editor and Features Editor (lots of free lipsticks!) on* Just Seventeen, *and Editor of* More! *and* Bliss *magazines. She loves drawing and writing and is a keen saxophonist and flute player. Right now she is a freelance writer contributing to* Elle, New Woman *and* Red *magazines.*

She says: "I'd written a few love stories for Just Seventeen *in the mid-Eighties, but I'd never written for children until I had Sam and Dexter. Having the boys prompted me to dig out books from my childhood (a big favourite was John Burningham's* Harquin the Fox). *As I read them I was amazed how – even though I'm ancient now – I remembered them almost word for word. I thought, if I'm going to write stories as exciting as these, I'd better start practising!"*

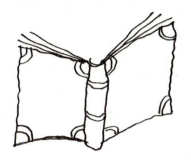

Aisha and Her Golden Fish

SARA MASON

Illustrated by

PETER BAILEY

L ong, long ago, before any of us here were born, there was a sunny continent called Africa. In the dead centre of West Africa, there was a small village called Nupe.

Now the king of this village was known as King Fula. He lived in the white palace with his numerous wives, children, courtiers and servants. All of them would sing to him and sing his praises. They sang to the beating of the drums, accompanied by men and women wearing the royal colours and dancing or performing acrobatics. The women would tie wrappers around their waists and their heads. Their wrappers were long pieces of woven cloth with bright colours, and gold and silver thread woven into the fabric. The king's colours were blue and green; all the members of the palace household wore the king's colours.

Nupe was only a small village and yet Aisha's house was the smallest in the whole village. It was nothing more than a hut. Aisha was an orphan. She lived in the small ramshackle hut with her only living relation, an aunt. Aunt Kunbi used to try to sell provisions in the market, like salt fish and agussi seeds. They were very poor. Aisha never minded being poor, in fact she never knew she was poor. Aisha had two golden fish that she kept in a small clay pot. Because she was the only person she knew with golden fish, Aisha thought she was very rich indeed. She gave her two fish names, and would spend hours looking at them swimming in their pot.

One season, when Aisha was nine, the weather was particularly bad. Day after day ... there was no rain. The harvest never came. Each day, the people would wait for the harvest to come but it never arrived because of the drought. There was drought in all the land. The people were all starving. There was no food to be had. Even those with money had nothing to buy in the market-place. The traders all stood around looking gloomy, bemoaning their fate and the lack of rain. The only people who had anything to eat were those prepared to travel to the neighbouring country. But the journey was long and dangerous, and many were afraid to undertake it. They preferred to wait and hope for the harvest to arrive.

Even the mighty King Fula in his white palace had nothing to eat. He had nothing to feed the royal wives, the royal children and the royal servants. Finally, one day, the royal king summoned his army to go into the village, to knock on every door and to demand food from the people. The people could not let the king starve! "Get whatever foodstuffs they have and bring them back to me!" King Fula insisted. "If anyone refuses, arrest him!"

So the army marched off into the village singing a war song to encourage themselves, as they felt pretty downhearted. They sang a traditional war song sung by warriors when they went into battle. This song made them feel strong, courageous and war-like. They sang and they felt much better singing their song, accompanied by the beating of the drums as they marched down the streets.

When they got to the first house they knocked, rat-tat-tat, on the door. "Hello! Hello!" An elderly woman came to the door. "Yes?"

"The king declares he needs whatever food you have; the palace is starving!"

"Oh sirs, I have only a couple of plantain and some dry garri."

The soldiers pushed their way into the woman's house and took all the food she had. They went outside and loaded up their cart with the poor old woman's food.

Then they knocked, rat-tat-tat, on the door of the second house. A woman answered the door. "Hello!"

The soldiers stared stupidly.

"Yes, what do you want?"

"The king declares he needs whatever food you have; the palace is starving!"

"Oh gentlemen, I have seven children to feed and all I have in the whole house is these few loaves and some sweet potatoes!"

"Ah, how very fortunate!" the soldiers said. "We like sweet potatoes."

"Oh, please! I beg you! My children will

starve!" The woman threw herself down on the ground. "I have seven children to feed."

"Out of my way, woman!" The soldiers pushed past her and piled their cart high with her food. The woman wept and wailed to no avail. The soldiers had already gone to the next house.

In this way, the soldiers went around the village, knocking on every door, plundering all the food they could find, with no thought for the poor villagers.

Aisha's hut was at the very edge of the village. At last they arrived in front of her door. By this time, their cart was piled high and overflowing with food. They knocked, rat-tat-tat, on her door.

"Hello!" Aisha came to the door.

"Hello, little girl," the soldiers said. "Where is your mother?"

"My mother is dead. There is only my aunt, but she has gone out. How can I help you?"

"The monarch declares he needs whatever food you have; the palace is starving!"

"Oh, I wish I could!" Aisha cried. "But there is no food at all in this house; my aunt has gone out to find some."

The soldiers did not believe her and pushed their way in to search. At last they saw the two golden fish. "Ah, these will do, the king will eat these between two slices of bread!"

"Oh, no, please don't take the fish, they are my pets!" Aisha cried.

The soldiers ignored her and put the clay pot on the cart and went back to the palace to eat all the good things they had stolen from the villagers.

Aisha threw herself down on the ground and wept bitterly. She prayed to the great god of blessings, Iguna, to help her. She prayed and sang, "Oh Iguna, oh Iguna. Iguna, Iguna, please. Oh Iguna, hear my cry!" Her voice was quite pleasant and tuneful as she sang.

The local people believed in the tradition of the great god, Iguna. Iguna was Lord of the wind, the rain and the harvest. He came accompanied by great gusts of wind, dressed completely in white. He was so tall that you could never see his face, it was always hidden in the clouds above the earth. No one has even seen Iguna's face. Well, not in this life, anyway ... not to my knowledge.

So Aisha prayed. Iguna was not deaf to her prayers. He was moved by Aisha's beauty, and the simple love she had for her golden fish.

He came down to Nupe in a huge tempest and sand storm. He literally blew Aisha over to the great white palace. She knocked at the palace gates. A swirl of dust and a cloud of sand passed in front of Aisha and blew the heavy palace gates open. Seconds later the roof of the palace flew completely off.

The king and the courtiers looked astonished. They stared in wonder. Aisha was blown to the king's side. The king seemed truly amazed. He looked up and saw Iguna standing there. Then King Fula said, "Oh great Iguna, you've been a long time coming! It is good to see you. It has been a terrible year; there has been absolutely no harvest. I've had nothing to feed the royal wives or the royal children. We've all had a terrible time. Where have you been?"

Iguna was very angry. He blew and blew; the courtiers trembled. Then Iguna spoke in a voice so loud it thundered in all the regions of the land. His voice was heard way over in East Africa.

Even the lions, tigers and elephants in Kenya heard Iguna's voice and trembled as he shouted, "BE QUIET, FOOLISH KING FULA! I have not come here for your sake. I have not come for the royal wives or the royal children. I don't care about any of them. I have come for the sake of Aisha. I have come for the sake of the people whom you have oppressed and stolen from. Starting today there will be two months of rain, the harvest will come and food will be plentiful... But as for you..."

Iguna snapped his fingers and the king disappeared. Then Iguna made Aisha into the queen. All the people danced in front of her. She was the youngest queen ever to rule this land, just nine years old. Aisha made her Auntie Kunbi into Prime Minister and Head of the Army. She chose orange and pink, just like her fish, for her royal colours. And she found her treasured clay pot with her two golden fish. When she looked in the pot she saw there were three fish...

Legend has it that the third fish was King Fula. Aisha never held that against him; she treated him with as much love as her two other golden fish. She ruled her people for many years. There was always peace in the land and food while Aisha was queen. And the people sang the queen's song to her all the days of her life.

SARA MASON

Sara Mason is an actress, theatre Artistic Director, theatre Workshop Leader and a playwright and translator. As well as appearing in films and on television, she has acted with the Royal Shakespeare Company and Steven Berkoff and has set up her own multi-cultural theatre company, Allegresse. Even with this dynamic career she has still found the time to write, having work published in Adam's Apple *magazine. She is a member of the British Actors Equity and loves going to the theatre and travelling abroad. Sara lives in London with her husband, poet Efosa Ebowe, and two-and-a-half-year-old daughter.*

She says: "In January, as part of their book week, I was invited to do a workshop at Queenswell Junior School. This turned into an African Storytelling Workshop as I work with an African drummer. Not used to doing things with seven- to eight-year-old juniors, I had to find an African story to use. But all the ones I found were too frightening, too gory or too viscereal for seven-year-olds. So I decided to write my own, and that's how Aisha and her Golden Fish *came about."*

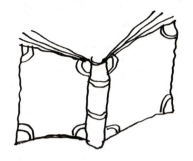

The Black Clogs of
Castle Doom

ROSAMUND ANNETTS

Illustrated by
PETER KAVANAGH

At about half-past eleven, just as the ancient tower clock tolled out twelve funereal strokes into the uneasy air, a man came rowing across Loch Dreirie to Doom Island, where the black bulk of Castle Doom towered high above the murky waters of the loch. He was a man with no name, and as he rowed he peered down anxiously from time to time at the oily black water. When he had almost reached his goal, a large bird flapped heavily over his head, landed with a plop on the stagnant surface and dissolved. The man with no name shuddered, and his teeth began to chatter as the keel of his boat ran ashore.

As he walked under the spiked portcullis, tiny bones crunched under his feet like gravel, and flocks of bats rose flapping around him. He pulled the bloodstained bell-rope nonchalantly, whistling to himself. As a viper slithered from under his heel, he told himself firmly that this was all in a day's quest.

The great door swung slowly open, and an aged retainer peered suspiciously round it.

"What you want?" he demanded.

"Apparently you do bed and breakfast," said the man with no name.

"Aye. Shut t'door, 'tis perishing cold. Single room?" enquired the retainer, leading the way to a large black register at a brisk hobble.

The man with no name stumbled blindly after him through the fetid darkness. "Splendid," he agreed nervously.

"Hang on while I lights candle."

"What a fine old place," said the man with no name, looking around him as the candle flared up.

"Happen. Name?" asked the servitor, clutching a broken quill pen in one palsied claw.

"I am the man with no name," said the man with no name proudly.

"Can't put that. What be t'name?"

"But I am the man with no—"

"If you got no name, you'll have to think of one."

"Certainly not!"

"How come you got no name, then? Did you never have one, or did someone take it away from you?" enquired the retainer curiously.

The man with no name flushed angrily. "It's people like you that take all the romance out of things," he snapped. "If you must know, my name is Eric."

"Eric, eh? Good enough name," grumbled the retainer, painfully writing "Eric" in the register.

Craning over his shoulder, Eric was not really surprised to see that the last entry in the book before his own name was dated 1893. "You don't seem to get many guests," he observed.

"Ah," said the retainer, with an evil smile, "there's many as rows this way across Loch Dreirie, but few goes back t'other way. I'll fetch t'lamp." He hobbled away.

Eric gingerly sidestepped a salamander with too many legs. As he waited in a noble attitude beneath the solitary candle, hair and teeth gleaming, some maiden with a love of the romantic might have likened him to a five-foot-eight blond rabbit in jeans. His intensely blue eyes attempted to sweep the hall with a calm and yet piercing glance, but failed, since as usual he had forgotten his glasses. He was examining an interestingly mutated spider when the ancient servant returned.

"This way, sir," he chortled as he bounded up the stone steps ahead of Eric with senile agility. "I hopes yer passes a pleasant night. Yer mustn't worry if yer hears funny noises in t'night."

"Funny noises?" said Eric. "What sort of funny noises?"

"Well, there be a lot of doors hereabouts as makes sounds strangely like the cries of helpless young maidens a-falling prey to ruthless blood-starved vampires," explained the servant. "Then there's the floorboard as sounds a bit like t'stealthy approach of a pitiless assassin. And of course—"

"That will be all, thank you," said Eric hastily.

"Good-night ter yer, sir," snarled the retainer, hobbling away.

Eric locked the door and put the dripping oil-lamp down on a rickety table. The walls were damp and stained, and the bed sagged in the middle. Eric removed a cockatrice's nest from a reasonably solid-looking chair and sat down.

"The man's appearance is rough," he mused, "but the coarsest rock may conceal a jewel. Perhaps I may yet be able to fulfil my quest without violence. Ooh, I do hate violence." A large toad croaked in agreement. Eric jumped several feet into the air, landing on the floor-board that made a noise like the stealthy approach of a pitiless assassin. It made it. Eric hastily got off.

The door creaked open and a shadowy white wraith slid in. Eric turned pale. "But I locked it!" he protested.

"Locked doors cannot keep out nothing," moaned the spectre, wringing its cloudy hands.

"Grammar," said Eric.

"Impudent boy, dare you correct my grammar?" cried the spectre, abandoning its moans. "I meant what I said. Nothing cannot be kept out. Only Something can be kept out. I am nothing, since I do not exist. Mine is the freedom of every locked door and solid wall. I pass freely through the bricked-up cloisters where once— "

"But I saw you open the door," interrupted Eric, who had been digesting all this slowly. "If you are nothing, you should just come straight through."

"Oh, shut up. I have come to chill your blood with a terrible warning."

Eric waited politely.

"I know who you are," declared the ghoul, resuming the grand manner. "You are Prince Eric of Swindon, and you are come to rescue the lovely Lady Arabella. Instead, you will not live to see the light of another day. Many men row across Loch Dreirie to Castle Doom, but few return. . ."

"You talk like that fellow downstairs," said Eric, his lip trying valiantly to curl. "Anyway, that's all wrong. I'm not after the lovely Lady Arabella at all. I didn't even know there was a lovely Lady Arabella. I'm on a quest to Milton Keynes to buy a birthday present for my mother-in-law."

"A likely story!" cried the spectre. "Disregard at your peril the warning of the Grey Lady of Castle Doom!"

"Grey?" said Eric. "Looks like off-white to me."

"You choose to ignore me! See then for yourself the fatal – aaaagh!" A mighty thunderclap like the crack of Doom itself shook the castle.

"Sit down for a minute," advised Eric kindly. "Put your head between your knees. Thunder can't hurt you."

"Drop dead!" spat the ghoul furiously, and swept through the door, slamming it behind her.

"But it's already closed, so how can she slam it?" wondered Eric aloud. He began to clean his teeth over the green, slimy washbasin.

In a dark corner of the castle where the reptiles and other crawling things were half-blind from lack of daylight, the evil Doomlaird paced slowly up and down a dusty gallery, thinking about his next murder, which was to be a particularly complicated poisoning. He was a tall man, and gaunt; he wore black velvet, with white lace ruffles, and he preferred to sleep in a large coffin lined with white silk, surrounded by black candles. He was not in fact dead, or even undead, but alive. Over the years, however, he had come to the conclusion that people who were alive did not inspire enough spine-chilling terror.

Far down the gallery a door creaked, and a man in a black mask appeared. He approached the Doomlaird and bowed. "A young prince has come to rescue the Lady Arabella, sir," he said respectfully.

"Sssssssssssssssssssss!" hissed the Doomlaird, his breath chill as the air that rolls from long-forgotten cellars. "Another!" He laughed, and the gallery echoed and boomed the sound back at him. "The Quark shall have this one!"

"I beg to bring to your notice, my lord, that you threw the Quark into the loch for biting your ankles."

"Oh yes. Well, we shall leave him to the Clogs, then."

"Sir."

"His name?" enquired the Doomlaird carelessly, examining his long pointed fingernails.

"Prince Eric, sir."

"Eric?" The Doomlaird sucked in breath with a snarling gulp. "Eric? I know that name. Tell me, is it not Prince Eric of Swindon? Only son of King Graham Thompson?"

"That selfsame, master."

"Curse him!" cried the Doomlaird, sending the creeping things scuttling for cover. "Curse him!"

"Certainly, sir."

"Can you not know of the deed his father did?" exclaimed the Doomlaird. "That deed that doomed me for ever to wander in darkness?" He went on without waiting for an answer, "Well, I'm not telling you. Go and let the Clogs out."

"Sir," said the servant, bowing low, and hastened away on his errand.

While this conversation was taking place, Prince Eric of Swindon, formerly the man with no name, was reading in bed. The sheets were damp and mildewed; they smelt of earth, and were the colour of rotten ice. Eric noticed none of this.

When the reptiles that infested the bed slithered on to his book he pushed them off and went on reading. After a while a secret panel in the wall slid open and an icy gust of wind entered the room. Eric did not look up.

"I told you so!" announced a self-satisfied spectral voice. "But did you listen? No! They never do!" The Grey Lady smoothed her transparent draperies complacently. "I suppose now you want me to get you out of this mess? Well, it's far too late for that!"

"Oh, it's you again, is it?" remarked Eric unencouragingly. "I hope it's something important." He continued to read.

"Don't you wish to know of the dread terror that stalks ever closer along the still cloister where no man walks?" enquired the spectre.

"If I must," yawned Eric. "How tedious your conversation is. Couldn't you cut down on the bricked-up cloisters?"

"For you, yes. But you must pay attention." (Eric reluctantly put down *Teach Yourself Icelandic*) "The evil Doomlaird knows that you are come to rescue the lovely Lady Arabella, and he has loosed upon you the dread peril of the Black

Clogs of Castle Doom." The spectre paused expectantly.

"But I don't want Lady Arabella, I keep telling you!" snapped Eric. "All I want is—"

"All right, I believe you. But that won't save you from the Clogs," the Grey Lady snapped back.

"What are these Clogs?" Eric demanded.

"Hark!" said the Grey Lady. Reverberating hideously through the castle came the sound of heavy footsteps. "They're coming!" she whispered. "The Clogs have haunted Castle Doom for many years, ever since a visiting werewolf left them behind."

"I didn't know werewolves wore clogs," said Eric.

"In the shower. They're afraid of verrucas."

"Oh."

"No man hears the Black Clogs coming save him outside whose door they are to stop. He who is destined to be found the next morning stiff and cold in his bed, his eyes starting from their sockets in terror..."

"Ooh 'eck!" gulped Eric, trying to cling to the Grey Lady, but being thwarted by her insubstantial nature. The heavy footsteps were grow-ing louder.

"Just a pair of clogs?" whispered Eric, backing up against the wall. "No wearer?"

"No," answered the spectre in hollow tones. "Just a pair of ghastly black clogs, striding eternally through the dark corridors where once —"

"Cut that out!" Eric warned her. The foot-steps had turned the corner. Eric seized a toad and clung to it despairingly as they trod up to his door and stopped.

"Help!" gasped Eric.

"There is no help for you now!" hissed the Grey Lady.

The door swung open.

The world seemed to freeze on its axis as Eric, paralysed by fear like a bird fascinated by a snake, beheld the dreaded Black Clogs of Castle Doom. Merciless and terrible they crouched on the threshold, a loathsome parody of everyday footwear. Whether the rest of his life lasted a second or a century, he knew that he would never be able to forget or indeed forgive that vile, abominable two-tone suede...

"Wait a minute!" said Eric indignantly. "They're not black! They're sort of chocolate and nasty mustard-colour!"

"Black sounds better," said the Grey Lady angrily. "Now look what you've done. You've destroyed all the suspense."

Eric took another look at the Clogs, which continued to squat hideous and motionless on the threshold.

"Well," he said nervously, "what do they do next, and when do they start doing it?"

"They don't *do* anything else. You're just supposed to die of fright when you see them."

"Oh, no! How pathetic!" said Eric, in disgust. He put down the toad and approached the Clogs. "Sure they don't do anything else?"

"Quite sure," said the Grey Lady resentfully. Eric picked up the Clogs and eyed them thoughtfully.

"May as well make some use of them," he said, throwing them into his suitcase. "Now I needn't bother going all the way to Milton Keynes."

"You can't do that!" exclaimed an indignant voice. The Doomlaird of Doom was lurking angrily in the corridor with his chief henchman.

"Come here," ordered Eric. "These clogs are a swindle. They're completely unfrightening, and they aren't even black."

"You fool!" shouted the Doomlaird rather unreasonably at his henchman. "You've done it now! The castle legend clearly states that whoso surviveth the peril of the Black Clogs must wed the lovely Lady Arabella."

"It always worked before," muttered the henchman sheepishly.

"But I'm married already," began Eric, then stopped and stared suspiciously at the Doom-laird, who was shifting from foot to foot. "I don't believe there is a lovely Lady Arabella," he said. "There isn't, is there?"

The Doomlaird looked at his shoes. "No," he muttered.

"I'm not staying in this crummy place a moment longer," said Eric disgustedly. "I'm going home."

The henchman plucked at the Doomlaird's black velvet sleeve. "You're not going to let him get away, are you?" he pleaded. "Remember the wrong his father did you!"

"Oh? What wrong was that?" Eric asked, folding his face-flannel.

There was a painful pause, while the Doom-laird thought frantically.

"I see," said Eric. "That's another load of lies, is it?"

The Doomlaird's face turned purple, and he looked around for something to hurt. His eye falling upon *Teach Yourself Icelandic*, he viciously squashed a few reptiles with it.

"Give that back," said Eric severely, and snapped his suitcase shut. "I'm off. And I think you're all utterly pathetic." He seized his book and strode to the door. On the threshold he paused, wondering whether he had been too severe. "I'll send you all invitations to my mother-in-law's birthday party," he conceded.

At about midnight, just as the ancient tower clock tolled out forty-three funereal strokes into the uneasy air, a man went rowing back across Loch Dreirie from Doom Island, where the black bulk of Castle Doom towered high above the murky waters of the loch. It was Prince Eric of Swindon, and as he rowed he revised Vocabulary

23 from *Teach Yourself Icelandic*. "Skrök," he muttered to himself, as a small bat plummeted past into the oily black water and exploded. The suitcase at his feet struggled briefly. "Quiet!" said Eric, and turned the page.

ROSAMUND ANNETTS

Rosamund Annetts was born in London but now lives in Cambridge where she went to university. She was a university teacher before becoming a rep for a paper merchant. However, in 1989 she decided to go freelance and now works from home as an editor, copy-editor and translator. She likes to relax with gardening, riding, tennis and playing the oboe and the cor anglais (not all at the same time!).

She says: "If I think too hard about how other people think you ought to write for children, or what children are supposed to think funny, I generally end up writing something dismal and boring that everyone hates. I think that's probably because if you pretend that your mind works in ways that it doesn't, or try too anxiously to please everybody, it shows. It works much better for me if I write something that I really enjoy writing and then see whether other people like it, and that's exactly what I did with this story."

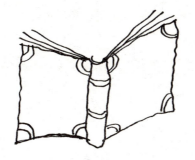

Ella and the Egyptians

B.J. Weir

Illustrated by
Jan Lewis

"We're doing the Egyptians this term," said Ella on the way home from school.

"Doing what to them?" said her mother.

"Learning about them. It's our topic. We're going to make a pyramid," said Ella. "And Miss says she's going to take us all to the British Museum to see the mummies. Parents can come too."

"I think I'm a bit busy at work right now," said Ella's mum quickly. "Where is Egypt then?"

"Is it in France?" said Ella.

Ella's mum sighed.

By Friday Ella had found out that Egypt was in Africa, and that the Ancient Egyptians believed in gods with animal heads.

"Isis and Osiris were brother and sister and they married each other," Ella announced.

"Were they being punished for something?" asked Ella's mum.

"No, I don't think so," said Ella. She loved her little brother Ollie even though he got on her nerves sometimes, but she couldn't imagine being married to him. "I think it's different for gods."

The next week Ella learnt about the River Nile.

"It flooded and made the land good for crops," she told her mother. "And they used to float dead bodies down the river."

"I expect that made it even better for the crops," said Ella's mum. "All those nutrients."

In the following week Ella wrote in her book about the pyramids: "The pyramids were for burying the kings. They put in everything they would need on their journey to the afterlife in with them, like food and money and jewellery and cats."

"And wives," said Ella's mum.

"Really?" asked Ella. "Did they kill them first?"

"Not always," said her mum.

Ella was shocked into silence, trying to imagine what it must have felt like to be shut up in a cold, dark tomb with your dead husband for company. "Yuck!" she said after a while, and went out to ride her bike.

Later that term the class started to write in hieroglyphics. This was an improvement on the handwriting of some people, and Ella enjoyed thinking of pictures to use instead of words. All the class had to write a note to take home asking their parents' permission to go on the museum trip. Fortunately, the note was translated into English on the back, because Ella's hieroglyphs completely baffled her mother.

"Why have you put a cooking pot in?" she asked Ella.

"Show me," said Ella.

Ella's mum pointed at a cauldron-shaped splodge.

"That's a money-bag," said Ella. "We need to

take two pounds fifty by Friday so Miss can book it."

"And a pillow?"

"That's not a pillow, it's a bag of crisps. We have to take a packed lunch."

"I know what those are," said Ella's mum, pointing at two jars. "They're the jars for putting the lungs and the liver in, when they were turning people into mummies, aren't they? Embalming jars, they're called."

Ella looked at her mother. "Don't be silly," she said. "That jar's peanut butter and that one's honey. It's what I want in my sandwiches."

"Yuck!" said Ella's mum.

Ella's mum and Ollie went to meet Ella off the coach on the day of the school trip. The children filed off the bus talking and laughing, looking hot and sticky. The teachers looked hot and sticky, too.

"Did you have fun?" asked Ella's mum as she held the car door open for Ella to scramble in the back.

"Oh yes!" said Ella.

Ella's mum waited. There was a long silence.

"Well, tell me about it," prompted Ella's mum.

Ella pondered. "The mummy cases were good," she said, after giving it some thought. "And there was some jewellery and stuff. And massive statues – huge, enormous arms made out of marble and stone. And there was a real, live mummy."

"A live one?" asked Ella's mum, in some alarm.

"Well, not really alive," conceded Ella.

"But really real?" said her mum.

"Yes. It was a man, they found him all curled up where he was buried in the sand hundreds and thousands of years ago. He was all brown and dried like an old carrot, and he even had bits of hair still stuck on his head," said Ella with relish.

"Was that the best bit then?"

"No. The best bit was the shop."

"Of course," said Ella's mum. "What did you buy?"

"A pencil-tin made like a mummy-case, and some scarab sweets and a thing to make an Egyptian boat. Will you help me with it?" asked Ella.

"Daddy's better at that sort of thing," said Ella's mum.

In the back of the car, Ella's brother Ollie hit Ella on the head with his rabbit, Squeaker, so-called because he squeaked when his tummy was pressed.

"Stop it, Ollie," scowled Ella.

"Don't fight, Ella," said her mum.

"I'm not fighting, Ollie is," said Ella.

"It's only because he's pleased to see you. He missed you today," said Ella's mum.

Ollie showed Ella how much he missed her by hitting her again. Squeaker's squeak caught her a blow on the back of the head, which made Ella's eyes water.

Ella gave Ollie a hard look. "I'll mummify you," she growled.

Squeaker came sailing through the air again. This time, Ella grabbed the rabbit and pretended to throw it out of the car window.

"Whoosh! There it goes!" she said to Ollie. While he peered out of the window, Ella hid Squeaker in her school bag.

"Squeaker all gone," said Ollie, looking puzzled. He thought about crying, but Ella gave him the last of her scarab beetle jellies from the museum and he cheered up.

Ella found Squeaker when she was packing her bag for school the next day. She frowned when she remembered Ollie whacking her and then the frown changed to a smile; she hesitated slightly before shoving the rabbit back into her bag and putting her lunch-box on top of it.

The end-of-term assembly was the next week and it was to include a demonstration by Ella's class of the work they had been doing on the Egyptians. Ella had been unusually secretive about her part in the assembly. Normally, Ella had to be a reader because she had a clear and loud speaking-voice, but this time, she told her mother, she was going to show something she had made.

"I have to hold it up and say something about it and then sit down again," said Ella.

"What is it, a picture or something? Not more hieroglyphics?" asked her mum.

"Just something I made. You'll see it when you come. You are coming, aren't you?"

"Yes, I said I would. Go to sleep now."

Ollie was having trouble going to sleep without Squeaker.

"Squeaker's lost, Ollie," said his mum. "I've looked and looked – in the car, under the bed, everywhere. What is it, Ella?"

Ella blushed. "Nothing, sorry. Night, Mum. Night, Ollie," she said.

Ollie still whinged and Ella's mum was cross. "Honestly, Ollie, we go through this every night. What about cuddling flopsy ted or panda tonight?"

Ollie eventually went to sleep clutching panda, but only after Ella had read him three *Thomas the Tank Engine* stories. For once, she did it without complaining.

Ollie and Mum arrived late for the assembly and had to sit right at the front, on the baby chairs. They were late because Ella's mum had had to hunt through the house for the camera.

"I always forget it, Ollie. This time I want a picture of her doing her bit in assembly."

When they sat down, Ella's mum took out the

camera and fiddled around, trying to get the class into focus.

Ollie waved his fat hands when he saw Ella. "Ella!" he shouted. He wriggled and Ella's mum twisted round to get a better grip on him and accidentally took a picture of the woman sitting behind her. Ella's mum apologized and Ella giggled and blushed, and tried to look serious. The headmaster came out to the front and told the parents that Class 3 were now going to present the work they had been doing on the Ancient Egyptians.

"The children have been working very hard this term," said the headmaster, "and I know they're looking forward to telling you all about the Ancient Egyptians. Who knows, we may all learn something. Now, just before we start, if any babies start to cry please take them outside so they don't distract the children. All right? Let's begin."

A small boy in Ella's class stood up, and read very quickly from the card he was holding in his hand. The words "Pharaohs" and "pyramids" were heard clearly, and a red-faced trio of children began to file from the back of the stage towards a fourth boy who was lying near the front and trying not to giggle.

"Our great Pharaoh has died and we must bury him in the proper manner," said one child.

The "Pharaoh" was heard to snort and had gone a very healthy red colour.

"Here are the things he needs on his journey into the afterlife," said a second child, placing a wine bottle, some plastic fruit and a string of red beads down next to the pharaoh.

"We will place him in a tomb which befits a great king," said the third child. This was the cue for something to come swaying down from the ceiling. As it came nearer, it was revealed as a cardboard pyramid. The pyramid landed with a sudden thump, leaving the dead Pharaoh's feet sticking out at one side. This was remedied by dint of shuffling feet and pushing the pyramid, and the scene was applauded loudly by the audience.

The next part of the assembly was about the Rosetta stone. Two small girls explained that they had seen the stone when they went to the British Museum and they had learnt that this stone had provided the key to understanding

the Egyptian hieroglyphs found on tombs and temples.

Ollie was not very interested in the Rosetta stone – he was bored and restless and starting to fidget. Ella's mum hoped she wouldn't have to take him out before Ella did her bit.

Suddenly, Ella was standing up and speaking to the audience. Ella's mum put the camera up to her face and tried to focus.

"The Egyptians preserved dead people by a process of mummification – that means turning them into mummies. They would take out organs like the brain and the lungs and the liver and then they would rub the body cavity with salt and spices. Then they would wrap the dead person in bandages. Sometimes the Egyptians would do this to animals as well."

Ella held up an object and said, "Here is one I mummified earlier."

Some of the parents laughed. Ella's mum gasped as a familiar figure swam into focus. Long ears, stumpy legs and a white cotton-tail poking out of the bandages at the back...

"Squeaker!" shouted Ollie.

Everyone turned to look at Ollie, and then

again at Ella who blushed and avoided catching her mother's eye. More people laughed this time. Ollie bounced up and down on Mum's knee, and the camera shutter clicked and whirred.

"Why didn't you just tell me you needed something to turn into a mummy?" asked Ella's mum, after school.

"You wouldn't have let me have Squeaker, would you?" said Ella.

"No. It belongs to Ollie. But there might have been something else you could use."

"I looked. There wasn't anything. Squeaker was the right size and I was only borrowing him," argued Ella.

"Well, as long as Ollie's got him back. He doesn't seem to mind, anyway."

Ollie was contentedly sucking the rabbit's ears in the back of the car. Squeaker's ears tasted of cinnamon and ginger, his stuffing was a bit lumpy and his fur was squashed from the bandages tied round his middle but otherwise he seemed none the worse for having been mummified. Except that somehow his squeak had disappeared.

"I expect it came out when I was embalming him," said Ella. She looked at Ollie, who was sleeping in his baby seat, rubbed the back of her head and looked out of the window as they drove home.

B.J. WEIR

Belinda Jennet Weir (to give her her full name) was born in Aberdeen and now lives in London with her partner and two children, Jenny, nine and Oliver, four. She has an MA in Social Sciences from Edinburgh University but is on sabbatical leave for eighteen months studying for an MBA at Manchester Business School. Her job as Executive of Bromley Care Services, a charity working with people with mental illness, doesn't leave her much free time. When she does get a minute to herself, she loves gardening and reading and writing. She has always written as a child and confesses to having won a Puffin Post competition some years ago, when she was presented with a badge by Alan Garner. She still hasn't got over the excitement!

She says: "We moved eight times when I was young and each time one of the first things my mum did was to march us off to the local library. I grew up with a love of books, and libraries and bookshops are still favourite places! My parents – father, stepfather and stepmother – have all written for publication so writing (for profit or pleasure) has always seemed natural."

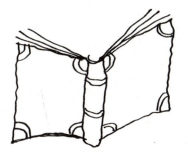

The Giant-sized Yuck

SIMON CHESHIRE

Illustrated by

ANTHONY LEWIS

The Scrubbings were a clean and tidy family, so they had a dreadful shock the day they were attacked by a horrible mountain of muck. It all began when they moved into their new house...

It wasn't actually a NEW house. It was very old and very creaky, but it was new to the Scrubbings. It stood in a smart street and looked quite germ-free from the outside. Nobody could have guessed what was lurking within.

Edward carried his baby sister, Emily, in through the front door, while Mum and Dad started unloading boxes from the removal van. Emily was a tubby little thing, and Edward thought he'd better put her down before his knees gave way. He was about to sit her on the floor by the stairs, when—

"Arrrghhhhghhh!" screamed Mum. "Don't put her there! It's FILTHY!"

She went so pale she almost vanished. Dad hurried in behind her. He screamed and went pale too. Luckily, he was ready with a box full of cleaning stuff, so that made him feel better.

"W-where can I put her?" grunted Edward. His knees were wobbling.

Mum looked around. "It's filthy EVERY-WHERE!" she cried. She gasped at the stairs, she shrieked at the ceilings, she wailed at the walls. Dad gasped and shrieked and wailed too. He pulled a tub of squirty soap from his box, and held it out in front of him, to warn off the dirt.

"This whole house is disgusting!" said Mum.

"Blurghh!" said Emily.

"I'm going to drop her in a minute!" said Edward. His knees were now wobbling like jelly that'd fallen off a cliff.

Mum tried to keep calm while she decided what to do. She breathed deeply, and shut her eyes for a moment, then snapped her fingers and pointed at Dad.

"Father, get the furniture out of the van and pile it up in the front garden. Put newspaper down first. I'm not having my wardrobes touching grass. And cover it all in newspaper, too. I'm not having my sofa getting rained on."

Dad retreated carefully, making sure he stepped backwards into his own footprints, so that his shoes didn't pick up any more grime. Mum shivered at the thought that she might have touched something covered in terrible diseases, and turned to follow Dad.

Edward's knees buckled. Before he could stop himself, he toppled backwards and landed with a thud on his bottom. Or rather, he landed with a squelch. He didn't know what it was he'd sat in, but he didn't like the sound of it.

"Arrghhhhghhh!" screamed Mum. "Get up! No, don't move! FATHER! Get back in here! Pick this boy up and take him to a bucket of disinfectant!"

Edward was beginning to wish they'd stayed at their old house. Emily scrambled across Edward's stomach, which Edward found extremely painful. She also leant over and tried to write in the dirt on the floor, which Mum found extremely revolting.

"Blurghh!" said Emily.

Once Mum had stopped feeling unwell at the thought of germs, and once Dad had piled all their belongings up in the garden, it was time for action. Edward was sure that this would mean Mum giving everyone mops and brushes and telling them which bits of the house to scrub.

And he was right.

"Father!" called Mum. "Make sure you get that broom into EVERY CORNER!"

Dad jabbed fearfully at the layers of dust that clung to the living-room. He brushed it all out through the back door, holding the broom right at the end of the handle in case a speck of something horrid tried to touch him.

"Edward!" called Mum. "Scrape every bit of grease off that kitchen!"

Edward grumbled to himself about mums and slavery. His legs were sticking out of a cupboard. His arms were trying to reach a really nasty glob of goo that was stuck behind the cupboard door.

Every dollop he managed to reach was hurled out through the back door.

"Emily!" called Mum. "That brush is for doing the landing! You do NOT EAT IT!"

"Blurghh!" said Emily.

Mum put on her anti-dust mask, her rubber gloves, and the white overalls she'd bought from a place where they made dangerous chemicals. She hoovered the beams that held the roof up in the attic, she polished the wallpaper, she took up the floorboards and washed the central heating pipes. She filled twenty-six plastic bin liners with filth and flung them out through the back door.

Sixteen hours later, the house was spotless. There were no grubby finger marks on the woodwork, and there were no drips of slime coming from the water tank. The Scrubbings were very pleased with themselves.

Out by the back door, on the other hand, was a nightmare pile of muck. In this huge, smelly heap was every last bit of dirt that they'd shifted. They peered nervously at it through the kitchen window.

"It's a giant-sized yuck," shivered Edward.

"At least it's not in here any more," sighed Mum, relieved. "Father! Go and fetch all the furniture off the front garden! And wipe your feet on the way back in!"

The Scrubbings, being such a hugely clean and vastly tidy family, all had hot baths before they went to bed. Their house, their belongings and their bodily bits and pieces were all free from filth, and they slept soundly.

It was only when they woke up the next morning that Mum and Dad started screaming again. In his bedroom, Edward's eyes snapped open and he looked out from under his pillow.

During the night, the enormous pile of yuck by the back door had vanished. All the grime that they'd shifted the day before was back where it started.

Dad hid under the bed in terror. It turned out that a fluffy mound of dirt was hiding under there too. Dad changed his mind and ran out of the house and down the street instead. Mum simply held the bedclothes tightly around her and started whining like a cat stuck up a tree.

"Crumbs," said Edward, amazed.

"Blurghh!" said Emily.

The Scrubbings scraped and polished and washed and swept and brushed. Sixteen hours later, the house was spotless once more. Mum had got Dad to move all the furniture out again before they started, and then she got him to move it all in again once they'd finished. Then she got him to hoover it, just in case.

By the end of the day, they were exhausted. Especially Dad. The man who owned the local corner shop was delighted that the Scrubbings were going to be his neighbours: they'd bought every last dishcloth and bottle of cleaning fluid he had in stock, and then asked him to order some more in specially.

"What lovely people," he said to himself as he closed up the shop for the night.

Mum locked and bolted the back door. Outside, all the dirt was once again in a giant, stinky heap.

"A freak hurricane must have blown the door open last night," said Mum, "and blown all that ... horrible stuff ... back in with it. Father! Seal around this door with sticky tape! The windows too! Nothing will get through there tonight. Tomorrow, we'll burn all that ... horrible stuff ... and then this whole nightmare will be over."

She turned the dial on the washing-machine to "Stain Blaster", blasted all the stains in their clothes to nothing, then blasted them some more, just to be sure.

Edward reckoned that Mum's freak hurricane idea was just plain silly. He thought long and hard about the problem. Freak hurricane, indeed! The only possible explanation was that a passing gang of Mexican bandits had shovelled the dirt back into the house for a dare. He decided to keep watch that night, to catch them in the act if they returned on another dare.

The window of his room overlooked the back of the house. While everyone else was asleep, dreaming of unstained walls and beautifully clean lavatories, Edward kept watch.

He could see the lumpy, mouldy outline of the giant-sized yuck, standing tall and wobbly by the back door. He could see ... his Uncle George ... and a wheelbarrow full of Martians ... and...

Wait a minute, he was dreaming!

Edward awoke with a jump. It was morning. He cursed himself for falling asleep on the job. With a quick rub of his bleary eyes, he looked out of the window.

The yuck was gone!

"It's vanished!" yelled Edward. "All the dirt's gone again!"

"Mmm, good," came Mum's sleepy voice from across the landing. It went quiet for a moment.

"Arrrghhhhghhh!" came Mum's not-sleepy-any-more voice from across the landing. "Father! It's vanished! It could be back in the house!"

Dad didn't wait to find out. This time he ran straight for the street. He flung open the front door, and –

SQQUUEELLLPPHHHH-FFLOPP!

– the giant-sized yuck fell in on top of him.

"It was waiting round the front!" yelled Edward.

Dust, muck and other assorted nastiness splattered and crawled across the hallway. Dad's howls of horror were stifled by great big mouthfuls of stuff that used to live behind the cooker. The yuck began to spread out and separate into various blobs and lumps.

"Father!" screamed Mum from the top of the stairs. "Get out from under there at once!"

A whirling cloud of fluff rolled up the stairs and engulfed her before she could say anything else. She flapped her arms about and held her breath.

Edward and Emily retreated into Edward's room. Splats of gunge that used to lurk at the back of the radiators came slithering after them.

"It's all trying to get back to where it started!" cried Edward.

Little rivers of black grime snaked their way up the windows. Balls of dust and hair hopped around and burrowed into the carpets.

"Blurghh!" said Emily.

Edward had an idea. He pulled the sheets off his bed and started flapping them as hard as he could. Within moments he'd whipped up quite a breeze. Emily wasn't big enough to flap whole sheets at once, so she flapped a hankie instead.

Dust and fluff were blown back along the landing and down the stairs. The cloud around Mum blew apart and billowed gently around the light fittings.

"Edward Scrubbings!" cried Mum. "Those are your best sheets!"

"But this is an emergency, Mum! We're being attacked by a mountain of muck!"

This was no time to argue. Mum grabbed a broom and started beating back a floppy mass of slime which was trying to slide between the bath and the toilet. Dad, who'd battled his way out of the hall, connected up the garden hose in the kitchen and hid behind the sofa. Whenever he heard movement, he jumped out and fired squirts of water at anything that dared to dirty the living-room.

The Scrubbings fought bravely. Mounds of filth made tactical moves to take control of the bathroom and the wardrobes, but Edward valiantly forced them into retreat using sheets, brooms, and a roll of super-absorbent kitchen towel.

The giant-sized yuck gradually re-formed itself outside the front door. All the dirt rolled and wobbled out of the house and clung together into one huge heap once more.

"Father!" cried Mum, picking bits out of her hair. "Fetch the van! We'll take this ... horrible stuff ... to the incinerator right now!"

"Wait!" said Edward, peering closely at the yuck. "Look..."

The giant-sized yuck looked sort of saggy, and sort of sad. Edward was sure he could see a sort of mouth, where two old strips of crumpled newspaper wriggled unhappily together. Mum, Dad and Emily huddled at the foot of the stairs. Edward stepped forward.

The yuck shrugged what might have been its shoulders. Dribbles of grease ran from two torn paper plates, set like eyes into what was maybe its head. There was a long pause while it pulled itself together (literally). Finally, it spoke to Edward in a deep, gurgly voice:

"This is my home."

Mum had to bite Dad's hand to stop herself screaming again. Edward wasn't sure about the right way to reply to an enormous pile of yuck.

"It's our home now," he said.

The yuck sobbed. It wiped its paper plates

with a mucky old dishcloth, which made the plates even dirtier.

"Please let me stay," it begged. "I'm a good cook. The filth down my right leg spent years in that kitchen, watching food being got ready."

Mum had to bite Dad's other hand to stop herself being sick.

"I'm sure you *are* a good cook," said Edward, "but you're also a very large pile of foul-smelling crud. We couldn't have you in the house. Mum would be permanently in tears."

The yuck blew its nose loudly on a bin liner. Mum hid behind Dad in case it accidentally sprayed something nasty.

"I could keep the house clean," said the yuck. "Instead of lounging around the rooms like I used to, I could keep guard. I could eat any new dirt which turns up. The house would be spotless for ever."

Now that sounded like a rather good deal.

"Spotless?" said Edward with a smile.

"For ever?" said Mum with an even bigger smile. "Perhaps, er, we've been a bit hasty. I'm sure we can find room for, er, Mr Yuck here."

The yuck gurgled happily and slopped its way

into the hall. The trail of muck it left behind quickly caught up, and slid back around its legs. It tried to give Mum a kiss, but Mum put a paper bag over her head just in time.

Edward and Emily soon got used to their new housekeeper. The yuck patrolled the house, sucking up every speck of grime it could find, and loved every minute of it. Sometimes it would leave a smear of itself on the curtains by mistake, but normally it was pretty good at its job. It lived in a big bucket under the stairs, and it enjoyed watching the telly with the family. Edward had to switch channels when the adverts came on, in case anyone mentioned washing-powder, but normally the yuck kept itself under control, and remembered not to leak horrible substances all over the place.

Mum and Dad gradually came to terms with having the yuck around. They liked the fact that no dirt could escape the yuck's notice, but they still kept clothes pegs in their pockets in case they caught a whiff of its lingering pong. At least they learnt not to panic. When Emily came in from the garden covered in mud, Mum simply picked her up at arm's length.

"Never mind," said Mum shakily, trying to put on a brave face. "I'm sure the yuck will deal with it."

"Blurghh!" said Emily.

SIMON CHESHIRE

Simon Cheshire works in the marketing department of Books for Students, who supply schools and public libraries. He has been in the book trade since leaving university in 1985, including seven years with the wholesaler, Heathcote Books. Simon is a member of the Society of Authors and has written three Jeremy Brown *titles for* Walker, *and has another book* (They Melted His Brain!) *coming out next year. He has a one-year-old son and lives in Warwick.*

He says: "I've been writing since I was a teenager, but it was only after I turned thirty and realized that my mental age would never exceed ten, that I turned to children's books and finally found my natural habitat."

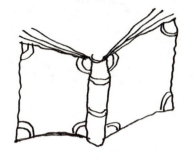

Sisters, Not Twins

JENNY SWANSON

Illustrated by
TANIA HURT-NEWTON

It isn't easy being a sister. Laurie and Lulu did not agree often, but they did agree on that. And it certainly isn't easy being sisters, if you look like twins when you're not. Laurie and Lulu had been born two years apart, but Laurie was small for her age, while Lulu was tall for hers. So they were just about the same size. Unluckily they also looked very alike, with long straight hair. Laurie's eyebrows were a little crooked, and Lulu's mouth was slightly wider, but you wouldn't notice unless you looked hard at them both. Which nobody ever did.

Because they were alike on the outside, people thought they must be alike on the inside. And they weren't. It caused all kinds of trouble. Some people also thought they should dress alike, and sent presents of identical clothes. Lulu didn't mind – she loved dressing like Laurie. But Laurie – well, she always wanted to look different.

Mum said shopping was a nightmare. When she took them to choose clothes, Lulu would never pick anything out. She waited to see what Laurie wanted, then said, "I'd like the same."

"If she's having that, I want something different," Laurie would say.

"So do I, then."

"You're a copycat! Copycat, copycat!"

Laurie would stick her tongue out and Lulu would cry. Often they would come home with nothing. Mum tried shopping alone, but if she chose clothes the same, Laurie sulked, and if she chose different ones, Lulu sulked. There was just no pleasing them both.

When Mum told the girls that they were to be bridesmaids, Lulu yelled, "Cool!"

But Laurie asked "What'll we wear?"

Mum looked at them sternly. "You'll be dressed EXACTLY alike. Bridesmaids always are."

Laurie and Lulu knew that voice – it meant

NO ARGUING OR ELSE. So they didn't even ask what the clothes would be like, just carried on eating. Lulu, crunching marmite toast, imagined something pink, with a long, full skirt, stiff petticoats, and a huge bow at the back. Laurie, nibbling cocopops, saw something short, sleek, perhaps lime green? Something which would miraculously make her look at least two years older than Lulu – and preferably three.

It was not to be. When the dresses came, they fitted perfectly and Laurie had to agree that they were lovely. There was just one problem: she did look EXACTLY like Lulu.

Lulu was deliriously happy: she looked so much like Laurie, that she even felt like Laurie. And secretly she had always wanted to BE Laurie. She thought that it just wasn't fair. She was sure she would have been a far better big sister – kinder, for a start. Laurie played with her quite nicely if no one else was there, but as soon as anyone else came along, everything changed.

The week before the wedding, Laurie invited a schoolfriend for tea. Victoria made up wonderful games in the playground, and Laurie really hoped they might be best friends.

"We're going upstairs," she shouted, as soon as they came in. "Don't let Lulu bother us, Mum."

Lulu sighed. She might as well be invisible when Laurie's friends were around.

But Victoria was different. She looked right at Lulu, not through her.

"Oh Laurie, let her come and play – it's more fun with three."

"YE-E-ES!" yelled Lulu, racing up the stairs before Victoria could change her mind.

"What shall we play?" she asked.

"Dressing up?" suggested Laurie.

"Boring," said Victoria. "Let's play witches."

Laurie wanted to say that that was dressing up, too, but Victoria was bigger than her, and she really, really wanted to be best friends.

"Okay," she said. "Lulu can be the witch and chase us."

"No," grumbled Lulu. "Let's all be witches."

"I know," squealed Victoria, "let's all be children. We can imagine the witch – she lives under your stairs. She's guarding a treasure of . . .

of ... of magic pinecones." She took some from Laurie's windowsill. "Hide these in the under-stairs cupboard, Lulu. We'll pretend that in here we're safe, but outside is all scarymagical. We'll take turns to go on secret missions to steal the pinecones."

It was the most thrilling game that Laurie and Lulu had ever played. They closed all the curtains to make it more frightening. The landing and the stairs were Scaryland, Mum's bedroom was Skeletonland, the bathroom was Witchy-land and the downstairs was Ghostyland. You had to be brave enough to visit each land in turn, before you could creep downstairs and sneak into the dark cupboard, to rescue a magic pine-cone from the Wicked Witch.

At first they fetched one every time. But then Laurie heard bones rattling in Skeletonland, and Victoria heard goblins whispering in Witchy-land. Mum was outside, and Ghostyland seemed lonely, and full of strange rustlings. They decided that they would only go downstairs in pairs, but even then it was creepy.

"I've had enough of this," said Laurie. "It's too scary."

"It's not!" cried Lulu.

"Come on," said Victoria, "don't be a scaredy-cat. All we need is some magic to protect us. Good magic."

"Like what?" asked Laurie suspiciously.

"Like the opposite of witches. Witches like black, and ugly things. So fairy magic should be white, and pretty sparkly things."

"We've got loads of sequins and bits of foil in the collage box," said Lulu eagerly. "If we scattered them on the ground, that might keep the goblins away."

Soon the carpets and stairs were sprinkled with little pieces of bright stuff. It did work, a little, but goblins still whispered in the bathroom, and now crocodiles snapped on the stairs.

"Now we'll dress up," decided Victoria. "Have you got any fairy dresses?"

"Laurie's got a frilly petticoat and a sparkly hairband."

"I'll have those," said Victoria.

Laurie looked at her, then fetched them out of the wardrobe. Victoria wriggled into the petticoat, adjusted the hairband and beamed.

"That feels much safer. What about you?"

"We haven't got anything else like that," said Lulu sadly.

"I don't much want to play," said Laurie. "I'll just stay here and guard the cottage."

"I want to play," insisted Lulu. "Come and look in my room."

They tiptoed across Scaryland and crept into Lulu's room. The wardrobe door creaked and Lulu screamed. Victoria peered into the wardrobe, then brought out a cream satin frock.

"This would be great."

Lulu was shocked.

"That's my bridesmaid's outfit. I can't wear that!"

"We'd only be in the house," tempted Victoria. "I'll wear it if you're scared."

"No – it's okay," said Lulu quickly. She remembered how marvellous it had felt when she'd tried it on. Surely that would protect her from the goblins.

She squirmed into the dress and tiptoed on to the landing. It worked. There were no scary rustlings at all.

"Now we need something for the crocodiles,"

said Victoria. "Something sweet, so they won't feel so hungry for us."

"Mum's got hundreds and thousands. Would those do?"

"Perfect. Run and fetch them, Lulu."

Lulu crept downstairs, her heart racing. She was careful to tread on the patches of carpet where the glittering papers lay thickest. Surely the magic would be strongest there. She dashed past the understairs cupboard and into the kitchen, snatched the hundreds and thousands from their shelf and rushed back. Laurie gave a shriek of horror.

"Lulu! Take that dress off this minute. And who said you could have the hundreds and thousands?"

"It's my dress," said Lulu sulkily, "so I can wear it if I like. Victoria said it was the right thing. And we're only going to borrow the hundreds and thousands, not eat them."

"Actually, I think we should eat a few," said Victoria. "Just to give us strength."

So they poured some into three dolls' saucers and licked it up. They did feel braver, so they refilled the saucers and left them for the crocodiles. Some spilled on the carpet, but Victoria said that was even better, and suddenly she took the lid off the container and scattered the rest of the hundreds and thousands over the top banister. They fell like rainbow drizzle upon the dark stair carpet. Laurie felt a lurch of excitement. The house didn't feel like their own dull, safe house any more. It was a truly magical land.

"I bet we could get to the bottom of the stairs in complete safety now," she said.

They tried it, and they could. Lulu laughed with joy.

"Good," chuckled Victoria. "Witches hate laughter."

"I know," squealed Lulu, "let's get rid of the witch altogether. Let's drive her out with a magic potion."

"Yes! If we all drink it at once, the witch will disintegrate," cried Victoria.

"There's Ribena in the kitchen," suggested Lulu. "Or milk?"

"I know!" cried Laurie. "Ribena IN milk. Like a magic milkshake. I'll get it."

She fetched three glasses, putting a large dollop of Ribena in each one and milk on top. It went a rich, dark blue, unlike any drink she'd ever seen before. She dipped a finger in and licked it. Plum! That proved it was magic – everyone knows that you can't make plums by mixing blackcurrants with milk.

They carried their drinks into the hall, then stood in a ring outside the cupboard door and raised their glasses.

"We must all drink at exactly the same moment," whispered Victoria. "If we get it wrong, the magic won't be strong enough. The witch will burst out of the cupboard and capture us. I'll count to three."

The others stood quietly, waiting. Lulu was so nervous that she felt sick. It seemed ages before Victoria began to count.

"One ... two ... three ... DRINK."

At exactly that moment there was a loud crash. The back door slammed and Mum came into the house. They all dropped their glasses. Laurie's and Victoria's fell on the floor, but Lulu's tipped straight down the front of her bridesmaid's frock. The dark blue stain spread across the cream satin.

Mum looked at them. She looked at the mess of blue milk and broken glass on the floor. Her mouth opened and closed, but no sound came out. It looked really weird and Lulu wanted to giggle. But she knew that she mustn't, mustn't, MUSTN'T, so she pinched herself hard to keep quiet. Laurie could hear herself taking deep breaths, but she didn't feel that she was getting any air.

Mum edged past them and looked at the stairs. At the torn paper scraps, the foil, the sequins and the hundreds and thousands smeared into the carpet. She looked back at the girls.

"I think I'll go home now," squeaked Victoria, and she did. She leapt past the broken glass, opened the front door and scuttled away, even though she was only wearing a petticoat and no shoes, and had not had her tea. Lulu supposed it was lucky that she only lived round the corner.

Finally Mum got her voice back.

"Lulu Cameron," she groaned, "that frock is ruined. You won't be able to be a bridesmaid. Laurie will have to do it on her own, unless I stay angry until next week – in which case neither of you will even be at the wedding."

.

Lulu burst into tears, but Laurie surprised herself. Her mouth opened and words seemed to rush out by themselves.

"We didn't mean any harm! You'll have to let us go to the wedding, or Aunt Clare won't have any bridesmaids. And I won't do it on my own. If Lulu can't, I won't. We're sisters, and we ought to be bridesmaids together. Can't you wash the dress? Please?"

"I suppose I shall have to try."

Laurie and Lulu had to have a bath, although it was not nearly bath time. Then they had to go to bed, although it was not nearly bedtime either. They lay quietly, listening to the scrubbing and muttering noises as Mum tried to sort out the mess. Luckily the carpet did clean up in the end. Unluckily, the dress did not.

Supper in bed should have been a great treat, but Lulu and Laurie sat in their separate beds, thinking that food had never tasted so dull and lumpy. Then they heard Grandma Laura's voice from the downstairs hall.

"Leave it to me," she said. "I'll take both dresses away with me, and I'll ring Clare. I have a plan."

Then the girls were able to settle down to sleep, because Grandma Laura had taken charge, and they knew that her plans usually worked out. Maybe they could still both be bridesmaids after all.

On the day of the wedding, Aunt Clare did have two bridesmaids walking behind her. They were very similar to look at, and their dresses were the same style, but different colours. One was cream, but the other had been dyed forget-me-not blue, and each had a sash of the opposite shade. Grandma had wired artificial forget-me-nots among the cream roses on both head-dresses, and both bridesmaids carried posies tied with blue satin ribbons. The hairdresser had trimmed the girls' hair, and it hung smoothly beneath the cream roses: waist-length on Lulu, but now only shoulder-length on Laurie. The haircut completely changed the shape of her face. She looked at least two years older than Lulu – maybe even three. A sister, but definitely not a twin.

At the wedding reception, the groom offered to make them a Ribena milkshake each, and all the grown-ups laughed when Lulu hid under the table. But it was a long time before either girl touched hundreds and thousands again.

JENNY SWANSON

Jenny Hughes Swanson is an academic and started life in Aberdeen before moving down to London. After graduating from University College London, she went on to Balliol College, Oxford to work for a Doctorate in Medieval History. From there she has carried out postdoctoral history research and held fellowships at Cambridge, Vienna, Paris, Munich and Sheffield universities; the Warburg Institute, University of London; and the University of Kent. She now works freelance from home in Kent and has published many academic articles and books. Jenny has two daughters, Kitty, ten and Charlotte, six. As well as medieval history and writing, she enjoys handicrafts, reading, music, country walks and swimming.

She says: "I've always made up stories as far back as I can remember, and when I was nine I began writing them down. I knew at once this was what I really wanted to do. It's always been children's stories as children have so much curiosity and enthusiasm. Through books they explore other lands, other times, other people's thoughts and experiences. By reading, kids access forms of language not used in everyday speech; no other activity offers this enrichment."

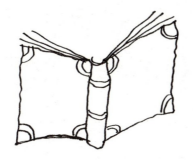

Sticky Bun and the Sandwich Challenge

JANET FRANCES SMITH

Illustrated by
SUE HEAP

Hello. The name's Sam. Sam Bun. My friends call me Sticky. Sticky Bun. Gerrit? And they think it's dead funny that my dad runs a sandwich shop. Jaws, it's called. That's because Dad makes great whopping sandwiches full of cheese, or ham, or cheese and pickle, or ham and pickle, or cheese AND ham AND pickle.

Doorsteps my gran calls them. Docker's butties my mum calls them. You have to open your jaws really wide to bite one of my dad's sandwiches.

This story starts when Maxwell Morris made fun of my dad. Make fun of *me*, yeah. Make fun of my big sister Mollie, yeah. But my dad?

No chance.

Maxwell's a big lad. He can crush Coke cans

with his head against the school wall. He's got a haircut as short as the grass on the bowling green and big, sticky-out ears like satellite dishes. I sometimes wonder when he talks to himself, if he's picking up Sky Sports or the Disney Channel and he can hear it in his head.

Maxwell Morris said, "Your dad couldn't make a sandwich to save his life."

"What?" I said.

"Your dad makes rotten sandwiches," said Maxwell.

We were sat at the packed lunch table in the school hall. In front of me was my old *Thomas the Tank Engine* sandwich-box from when I was in Infants. I'd picked off most of the transfer so that the other kids didn't laugh at me. Mum can't afford to buy me a new one.

Maxwell's is a posh new football lunch-box, signed by some of the players at Man U. Or so he said. I think David Beckham's signature looks just like Maxwell's writing, but I'd be daft to say so. Do I want a squashed head? No, thank you.

Anyway, he was biting into a Mega Munch Energy Bar and you could almost see his muscles rippling, when he said this about my dad.

"What's wrong with my dad's sandwiches?" I said.

Maxwell looked at my lunch. If sandwiches could blush, then this one ought to have done. I know that. But I still couldn't have this dung-head slagging off my dad.

"*My* dad says the bread's dry, it's marge instead of butter and you need specs to see the filling," said Maxwell.

The other kids on the packed lunch table stopped eating and looked at me. The bit of sandwich still in my mouth began to taste like the insole of our Mollie's trainers.

Maxwell's ears twitched. He had probably tuned into another station. Snooker maybe.

"Your dad's sandwiches are boring."

From the corner of my eye I saw Sylvie Sanderson look at me. She hated Maxwell more than any of us. Bag-of-spuds he calls her. Just because her dad runs the fruit and veg shop. And because she's a bit bigger than the other girls.

"Don't listen to him, Sticky," she said.

I felt the back of my neck start to go red. That was because of Sylvie. I felt my knees begin to wobble. That was because of Max. I cleared my throat and tried to deepen my voice.

"If we were in the playground," I said to Max, "I'd bash your head in." My deep voice must have got lost somewhere, because it came out in a squeak.

Maxwell laughed. You could see the huge gap where his front teeth had come out and there was spit and Mega Munch dripping in his mouth. It was like the cave of doom.

"*You* – bash *me*?" Maxwell bent his arms and did an impression of a Gladiator. He was right. Ever seen a stick insect? That's what I look like, except I'm not green.

"If your dad's so good at making sandwiches, why does he never have any customers?" sneered Maxwell.

"He does!" I said. But as the words came out I knew Maxwell was right. People came once. Twice maybe. But hardly ever again. That's why we didn't have much money at our house. Dad's sandwiches were boring. I should know. I had to eat them every day for my school dinner and the leftovers for my tea.

The noise of children in the hall sounded like

the roar of a hundred railway engines in my ears. But through the sound I began to hear a voice. It was Sylvie. "You'll show him, won't you, Sticky?"

"Will I?"

"You'll bring a great sandwich for your dinner tomorrow, won't you?"

"Will I?"

Then I looked across the table and saw her round face and pleading large blue eyes. And I found myself saying, "Yes. I'll show you, Maxwell Morris. You wait until tomorrow!"

Dad met me at the school gate when it was home time. He shut the shop early because there weren't any customers. It was the best time of the day for me. We'd play daft games on the way home. Dad would pretend we were from the Hole in the Wall Gang and that we had to get down the hill and past the chippy to our house without being spotted by the sheriff. That usually involved dodging in and out of people's doorways and we got some funny looks, I can tell you.

But I didn't feel like playing daft games. Dad tried. It was something to do with aeroplanes and going "Neeeiow!" down the street with our arms wide apart, but I didn't have the heart for it.

"What's up, son?" he said.

"Nothing, Dad," I said.

"When kids say 'nothing' it's usually 'something'," said Dad. He's clever like that. Not much gets past him. Except goals when he plays for the village team. But that's another story.

"Have you ever thought of making different sandwiches?" I said.

"Different?" He scratched the back of his head. "Sandwiches?"

"Yeah."

"You mean – not ham or cheese or pickle?"

"Yeah."

He needed time to think, to let the idea ooze into his brain. So I talked about the weather. He was looking at me as though my brains were cooked, but I still rattled on.

As luck would have it, Gran came for tea. Even my dad's face lit up when Gran came. It wasn't her as much as the shopping she always brought. "I'm not having stale sandwiches for my tea, our Pam," Gran said to my mother every

Wednesday. "Got you a bit of shopping. Bit of nice bread. Some eggs. Lettuce."

We had a nice tea but Dad was unusually quiet.

"What's up with you?" Gran asked him.

"Different," Dad said and gazed into space.

I saw Gran later, checking the empty beer bottles. But I knew that Dad was thinking.

The next day, I was flying round, getting ready for school, when Dad gave me my lunch-box.

"Different," he said and winked. I didn't have time to say much, just grabbed it and ran. As it was, the bell had already gone before I sat down at my desk. At lunchtime, I suddenly remembered. Sylvie sat nearby and raised her eyebrows at me like you do when you're asking someone a question. I opened my lunch-box and there, inside, was a large foil-wrapped parcel. I was still staring at it when Maxwell blustered in and sat down opposite me.

"So – what have we got today, Sticky Bun?" he sneered at me.

"Probably the best sandwich in the world," I said.

Sylvie looked scared. I went hot then cold.

"Let's have a look then, dung-head," said Maxwell.

I peeled back the foil wrapping while my heart did a tap dance in my chest. And then I gasped.

Inside the foil were eight neat, triangular sandwiches – not the doorsteps I was used to. I picked one up and peered inside. It was cream cheese, dotted with chives, topped with finely shredded lettuce and thin slices of ruby red tomato. I forgot about Max. I even forgot about Sylvie. My mouth felt wet. I bit into one of the sandwiches. It was terrr-iffic!

"They look good," said Sylvie. "Can I have one?"

I passed one to her.

Maxwell said, "What are those funny green bits?"

"See, I told you," said Sylvie, munching my dad's sandwich. "And I bet Sticky can bring a different sandwich every day next week."

I gulped.

"And the week after," she said.

I went hot and then cold.

"Hang on a bit," I mumbled.

But Maxwell had already begun to speak.

"Okay then," he said. "Two weeks. I'll give him two weeks. And each sandwich has to be different and bigger and better than the rest. Or else."

"Or else what?" I squeaked.

He did his impression of a Gladiator and grinned. At least the gap in his front teeth grinned.

"Course he can do it," said Sylvie. "After all, his dad runs a sandwich shop."

Dad wanted to pretend to swim home when he collected me from school. "We can pretend that you're a shark and..."

"No, Dad, listen," I said. And then I told him. All about Maxwell and what he'd said about my dad and about the shop and about the sandwiches. Everything. Even about Sylvie.

"Don't worry, son," he said.

"But I am worried," I said. Thoughts of Dad's stale grey sandwiches flooded into my brain.

"I'll do the worrying," he said. "I'm a dad. That's what dads do."

So he went to the library on Saturday and brought home some cookery books. He started making lists. And when I wanted a kick-about at the park he wouldn't come. Later on, I suggested going out on our bikes, but he said he was going to the supermarket. Weird.

Come Monday morning, I was flying round as usual, finding my reading book and stuffing my gym kit in my bag, when Dad came up to me, beaming all over his face. He had something behind his back.

Do you know what it was? It was an ace Man U lunch-box – bigger than Maxwell's.

"Good luck," said Dad and he winked.

Word had got round at school about the sandwich challenge. Loads of kids tried to cram on to my lunch table but Mrs Bones, the dinner lady, soon sorted them out.

But Maxwell managed to get near me. Sylvie was seven places away. My heart started bopping as the room went quiet. I opened my lunch-box. And there inside the foil parcel were turkey, tuna and tomato triangles oozing with salad cream. They looked terrific. They were terrific. Maxwell looked ticked off.

Tuesday came and when I opened my lunch-box, there were six double-decker pepperami, peanut butter and pickle sandwiches, with added pieces of pork pie.

By the end of the week – when I was tucking into cucumber, Camembert and coconut sandwiches, cut into the shape of footballs – even Mrs Bones began to take an interest.

"And what have we got today, Sam?" she asked me, taking a peek. And when she saw them she said, "Think I'll have to take a walk down to your dad's shop this weekend if he can make sandwiches like that."

Max nearly choked on his Mega Munch.

The weekend didn't go down too well. Word had got round. People were queuing outside Dad's shop when he opened up on Saturday morning. Instead of being able to close early and come down to the park with me, he was still serving customers at tea time.

The shop was shut on Sunday, but Dad hadn't got time for me then. He was either out shopping for some special ingredients or poring over cookery books.

I'd got one more week to do.

On Monday I had spicy sausage, soya sauce, sardine and sago sandwiches. On Tuesday I had cheese, chutney, chocolate and chive sandwiches. On Wednesday I had carrot, cress, cottage cheese and crisp sandwiches. On Thursday I had banana, bacon and blancmange sandwiches. And on Friday I had triple-decker chocolate chip, jam and jelly sandwiches.

And on Saturday – I was sick. My tummy ached, my head hurt and my legs felt like jelly. I never wanted to see another sandwich in my life.

Mum looked after me. Dad was too busy coping with the queues in the shop. Sylvie came to see me. She ate the grapes she'd brought me and told me Maxwell had stopped calling her names.

A reporter from the local newspaper came and told Dad he was in the running for the Super Sandwich award. A photographer took a picture of him, biting into one of his famous Cherry Chomper sandwiches.

When I felt a bit better on Saturday afternoon, I was watching the queue from my bedroom window. I nearly fell through the glass when I saw Maxwell's dad there.

But it was all getting a bit too much. Dad was flaked out on Sunday. "Exhausted, I am," he said.

"Come to the park, Dad?"

"Sorry, son – and I won't be able to pick you up from school tomorrow. Shop's too busy."

"Oh," I said.

"What's the matter, son?" he said.

"Nothing."

"When a kid says nothing he means something," said Dad. "What's wrong?" We talked then, me and Dad. Talked until tea time. And by then I was feeling well enough to try one of Dad's spicy sausage sandwiches. Nice it was, too. The next day, there in my lunch-box was a foil-wrapped parcel. The other kids crowded round. For once Mrs Bones didn't stop them. But when I peeled back the foil they all gasped.

Staring me in the face was a rather ordinary, boring cheese sandwich. Maxwell didn't say a word. Sylvie winked at me. And when school finished, there was Dad waiting for me at the gate, wearing a black patch over his eye.

"Pirates tonight, Dad, right?" I said. And we swashbuckled our way home, past the chippy, aboard our pretend galleon.

We popped into the shop before we went down to the park for the kick-about. Sylvie's mum was there in a bright green overall, laugh-ing with the customers. And Maxwell's mum was behind the counter too. Both of them were serving the never-ending queue.

Dad reckons, as he was the brains behind the whole thing, he deserves a break. So he leaves Sylvie and Maxwell's mums in charge at tea time and picks me up from school. Sylvie drops by most days, too. She joins me and Dad in the park. She's a great goalie.

And me? Oh, I have school dinners now.

Janet Frances Smith

Janet Frances Smith lives in West Yorkshire and has two daughters aged eleven and eight. She has been a journalist most of her life, working on several provincial papers and magazines as reporter, editor and feature writer. She has written a series of guide books and has also self-published a book called Labour Days *about having a baby before the birth of the NHS. A member of Calderdale and Kirklees Children's Book Group, she has been shortlisted for the Fiddler Award which is given to a first novel for children aged between eight and twelve.*

She says: "Fed on a limited diet of Enid Blyton as a child, I was unaware of the rich vein of material that was around even then. But since my own children were born, one of the parental tasks I have enjoyed most is reading to them and we have discovered some of the most wonderful children's literature available today. This fired my enthusiasm to write children's fiction myself.

"Children's authors are a generous breed and many have given me words of encouragement. But the best critics are my two children who have had to endure my first, second and third drafts until I get it right!"

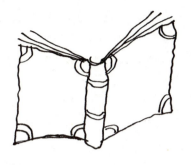

Snowy

JOHN NEVINSON

Illustrated by
IAN BECK

I'm always scared. Scared of everything. My big brother Phil says I'm frightened of my own shadow.

Scared of everything, big and small. I go the long way to school so I don't have to pass that big dog at number 27 or the crazy old lady with the cats at number 39 who plays her piano all night. But if I go the short way to school I still have to pass the Armstrong twins' house, and they sat me in the road once and pushed snow down my ears. The Farrell kids saw them and they've called me Snowy ever since.

And even when I get to school, I get scared. I stay away from the Armstrong twins in the playground, as well as the kids in the different gangs. I hide from a parent called Mrs Harrison because she says I deliberately took her Martin's lunch-box, but it was the same colour as mine and didn't have a name on, so it was a mistake.

Then when the teacher comes out for us to line up at nine o'clock, I don't want to be chosen to walk down the corridor to ring the In-Time bell for her, just in case I do it wrong, so I don't catch her eye by staring at the map of Britain painted on the ground.

All those dots on the map. G for Glasgow, N for Newcastle, L for Liverpool... Are there as many scared people living in each of those little dots? Are there lots of children just like me, all over Britain?

Then I get into school. I like so much of it but I can't enjoy it because I'm scared about things coming along that I don't like. I mean, we don't have swimming till Thursday but I worry about it even on Monday, and by Wednesday my stomach feels like a big achy hole. I'm not just scared of the water and the loud instructor with a face the colour of ham, but I worry if I'll be the last ready to get on the coach for school, so I struggle to get my socks on to wet feet, and they stick, and I panic, and people shout, "There's just one person still changing," to the teacher, and that's me, and I panic more... It's really horrible.

And it's not just swimming. Friday morning is spelling test and tables test. I usually get full marks but I'm always worried that I might not manage it. And I'm scared of looking after the class goldfish in case I have to clean the tank and might need to hold the slippery, delicate thing. And once I misread the thermometer and spoiled the whole class's weather records on temperatures.

My mum says, "Stop worrying." My dad just sighs. My brother Phil is a teenager so naturally says kind things like, "Don't be so wet, you wally!"

So I woke up yesterday and immediately thought of all the scary things which would probably happen today, Tuesday. No baths, no spellings. But we were having a visitor in to talk to us about animals, and my teacher said he'll have some in boxes or cages, and already I'm dreading that the visitor will say, "Hold this giant Indian spider," or let a hawk fly round the room, and it'll settle on my shoulder, and ... and...

Dad's car is away down the road as I get up. Phil is in the bathroom sploshing and gurgling before his usual mad dash to the school bus. Mum helps at the old folks' home, and leaves just after me, but she smiles as I check everything five times – packed lunch-box, hankie, reading book...

I get a peck on the cheek from her. A peck on the cheek reminds me of the animal visitor. Will the eagle or the vulture give me a real peck on the cheek?

I start to go the long way round, to avoid the dog at 27 and the crazy piano lady at 39, but then I see a large woman marching along a child with a green lunch-box, and it's Mrs Harrison who says I stole it, and I don't want to meet her, so my stomach does a big jump as I turn to go the other way to school.

I pass number 27, and there's no sign of that dog. I'm in luck, I think. It must be because it's the seventh day of the month, and seven is a lucky number. I reach the next danger spot, number 39.

This is where old Mrs Stewart lives. Her front garden is like a jungle of matted brown grass, and her straggly privet is too high for even my dad to see over. Late at night, she plays the piano loudly, no tune, just a thundering rumble. Her lights are on, the curtains open, but nobody can see her through the forest of hedge. Sometimes, Mrs Stewart just leans on her brush, looking up the road. Our Phil says her husband was killed in Hitler's war and never came home, but she looks up the road waiting for him to appear. It's sad, I should feel sorry for her, but I'm too scared of her to feel sad.

I've never heard a barking like it. I'm right outside number 39 and the dog from number 27 is suddenly there in front of me. It's a big brown Alsatiany-wolfy thing with huge yellow teeth and a slobbering pink tongue. He hates me. I think he knows that I was glad when he was knocked down by the ice-cream van last summer. I can still see the damaged fur on his back where he was cut. Roscoe, he's called, but I don't know why.

Roscoe snarls and moves towards me. I feel like my feet are glued to the pavement. My brain wants my body to move somewhere safe. Suddenly, I shoot into a dark patch of shady grass behind a high hedge. Safe. Even Roscoe won't come after me here. He slopes off, looking back and barking in disappointment.

I'm safe. Then I realize where I am. I'm standing in crazy Mrs Stewart's jungle. And I can hear a voice calling Snowy. That's the horrible name that the Farrells call me. But they're at school by now, so who can it be? Suddenly, out of the front door comes the mad old lady calling Snowy.

At first, I'm scared, as usual. Then I'm really scared. Have the horrible Farrells told Mrs Stewart my nickname is Snowy? Is everybody in this street against me?

Then I realize that the old lady is crying when she says Snowy. Big tears are rolling down her pink cheeks, and she pushes back her snow-white hair with an old veined hand. "Snowy, oh Snowy," she sobs.

Now, all at once, I feel so sorry for the old lady that I forget all the stories about her which Phil told to scare me. I go up to her, and say stupidly, "Snowy?" She turns her sad old blue eyes to me, and looks so confused and lost that I just find myself taking her old hand, and hear myself saying, "What's wrong?"

178

"Snowy," she says. How does she know that people laughingly call me that?

"Snowy," I say to her, because I can't think what else to say.

"Snowy?" she says again. Anyone listening to this strange conversation on the other side of the hedge would think we were crazy, Mrs Stewart and me.

But when she says Snowy again, I realize that she's not really looking at me, but sort of through me, like I was invisible. I find myself turning, and see, perched on the top of a rickety wooden shed roof, a dirty white ball of straggly fur.

"Snowy," she murmurs, and I say Snowy again because now I realize what the old lady is upset about. Her old cat Snowy is stuck on the rotten roof of the shed with his paw caught in a hole, and it's yowling away making noises like, "Maaaaa-am."

I find myself walking over to the metal dustbin, and hoisting myself on to it. (Me, who won't go on the climbing frame at school!) I can't reach the unhappy fur bundle, so I scramble back down, look through the dirty brown windows of the shed, and see a ladder in the gloom. I walk in. Mrs Stewart just watches me, still saying Snowy.

I drag out the ladder and prop it against the wall. The shed creaks as my weight comes against it, and the ladder complains, too. I get to the top of the steps and reach across the roof. Snowy spits and bats his open claws at me, and I notice a look of hate in his sharp green eyes. I also notice blood on his leg, caught in the hole in the roof, and see that each time he scrabbles to get free, he jams it further into the splintered space.

Now I'm on the roof and my feet have left the ladder which sways and falls with a crash into a bank of green nettles. The roof isn't nice and firm like a pavement, it sort of dinges in like the mattress on my bed. I feel quite sick. But with excitement. I'm amazed. I'm not scared at all. Everything is so unreal and like a dream. Me, up a ladder on the crazy lady's shed roof, rescuing her vicious cat, and I don't feel scared at all!

As I hear my voice say firmly, "Snowy!" I reach out and the terrified creature leaves a pattern of red scratches across my hand which start to ooze blood. But I'm determined to grab

Snowy before he slides through the hole in the roof, which is getting larger. I know if it falls through, the cat will be hurt, and perhaps break bones. I don't seem to have time to think about any bones which I might break.

All this time, Mrs Stewart has been moaning "Snowy". Now I suddenly hear a man's voice, sharp and Scottish, saying, "Stay still, don't move!" Before I can turn my head, I hear a swish of nettles as the ladder is pulled out of them, and a bang as it's pushed against the shed. A strong hand touches my foot, and the voice says, "You're okay. I'll see to this cat. Well done. It was a brave try."

In the next whirling seconds, the man has the cat, which seems too surprised to scratch him, and he puts it on the path. It scampers past Mrs Stewart, who follows it into the dark hallway of the house. The man helps me down the ladder. I don't know what to say to him. Perhaps I'm in trouble for climbing on the roof and damaging it, so I run past the white van which he must have parked outside number 39, and dash off to school. I mustn't be late, oh no, I mustn't be late. I'm always scared of being late.

I'm there just in time, but I'm so flustered and hot that the teacher on duty sees my scratched hand and gets the Welfare Lady to clean it. She wants to know what happened but I can't explain. I want to be in my classroom before the door closes, so I won't have to walk into the room in front of them all, and perhaps be late for the register.

I'm just in time. It's a rushed register because we're straight off to the hall to meet the visitor with the pets. The man who'll let the owls fly round and the tarantulas crawl over my hand.

I sit on the carpet. I look at the red scratch marks on my hand. I stare down. If I look up, I might catch his eye, and he'll say, "Now, you can help me with this big snake – come out here." I keep looking down. All the classes are in the hall now. The mumbles of excitement stop as our headteacher says, "Here today, with some wonderful furred and feathered friends, is Mr Sutherland."

As soon as Mr Sutherland speaks, I recognize the Scottish voice. I jerk my head up in surprise and look straight into his eyes. We stare at each other. We know each other. He smiles and walks towards me. When he says, "Come here," my feet obey him, and I'm standing in front of two hundred children. It's so quiet, all I can hear is my heart banging just below my throat. Can't everyone hear it thump? I'm sure they can.

The man takes my scratched hand. I hear some of his words jumbling together. "On my way here today ... child on a roof ... old lady pointing ... terrified cat stuck ... brave young person here ... scratched but determined to rescue it ... wonderful ... a really brave soul ... round of applause, please."

There's the growing wave of sound, claps, cheers. And I think, That's not for the netball team or the Good Work kids, that's for me. I find myself smiling broadly. I can pick out faces, really friendly, nice faces. The Farrells are grinning, and the Armstrong twins are jerking their thumbs up, and Martin Lunch-box is smiling at me... Everybody is looking at me, and do you know what? I feel GREAT.

The twins and the Farrells walk home with me. We pass Mrs Stewart's house. She's leaning on her brush, looking up the road as usual. She looks at me as if she's met me in a dream once, and half smiles, half nods. Her cat is weaving around her ankles.

"That's Snowy," I say, and the Farrells laugh. Everyone will still call me Snowy, but not in a nasty way any more.

Oh, I still worry about the baths and spellings and the big loud Juniors in year six, but the day I rescued Snowy made me feel that I was just a little bit special and quite brave, and it made me feel braver and better about myself. I'm proud they call me Snowy now!

JOHN NEVINSON

John Nevinson lives in Carlisle, but is originally from Liverpool, where he trained to be a teacher. He now does some supply teaching after taking early retirement in July 1997. As well as writing, his interests lie in cinema, theatre, fell walking and visiting historic buildings. He is also a member of the British Titanic Society and has traced his family tree back to 1723! Apart from two stories in the school magazine thirty-five years ago, this is his first published story. When he read it to his old class, they gave him a round of applause!

He says: "I think that a lot of children want to read about someone whom, if not exactly themselves, they recognize readily. Some authors seem to drop characters into adult problems like divorce, when I think most children want to explore themes which loom large in that important part of their time spent away from adults. A treacherous friend or a disastrous school football match can be the most traumatic experience!"

Children from these schools helped judge this year's competition:

Rosendale School, London

Eliot Bank Primary School, London

St Bartholomew's School, London

Collydean Primary School, Fife

Honiton Primary School, Devon

Fair Field Junior School, Radlett

Shirley Junior School, Southampton

Shirley Infant School, Southampton

Sinclair Infant and Nursery School, Southampton

Sinclair Junior School, Southampton

Mason Moor Primary School, Southampton

Do you want to read *more* of the best children's stories?

If you have enjoyed *Story of the Year 6*, then you'll love books 4 and 5, as well.

Story of the Year 4 is 1996's edition of winning entries. It is a brilliant selection of gems, with the shiniest being the magical and beautifully told winning story, *The Sheltie*. With nine more tales to choose from (including escaping eels and a house whose heart is fit to break) this selection is going to win with everyone!

Story of the Year 5 is the best of 1997's entries and what a collection it is. The winner is the heart-warming *Spare Bear*, but that's not all! There's great football and bad jokes; Hallowe'en hauntings and greedy guzzlings; poignant poetry, a prattling pigeon and lots, lots more!

Funny and touching, exciting and magical, these are the Stories of the Year.